"You Are Going Exactly Where I Take You. To My Kingdom."

Carmen shook her head, groped for breath. "I—I can't travel…my passport isn't valid.…"

"I don't need one to take you out of the country and into mine. My word is enough. Anyway, I'll arrange for one. It will be waiting for you when we arrive at my home."

"I'm not leaving *my* home."

"You are. In case you haven't grasped it yet, I am bringing Mennah with me. Since you are her mother, this means you come, too."

A hurricane of emotions started churning inside her. Trying to hide her upheaval from his all-seeing eyes, she tried to scoff. "I hope this isn't how you make your peace proposals. Your region would be up in flames within the hour."

He gave her a serene look. "I save my cajoling powers for negotiations. This isn't one, Carmen. It's a decree. You had my child. You will be my wife."

Dear Reader,

In a high-stakes situation that threatens the throne of a phenomenally prosperous desert kingdom, what would the kingdom's heirs do to defend it? I asked myself this question when THRONE OF JUDAR's premise was blossoming in my mind. And the answer? Anything, of course!

In *The Desert Lord's Baby*, Farooq has to secure the succession to the throne. And the key to everything is Carmen. The lover who dared walk out on him and kept his baby a secret. Claiming her will secure all his objectives—sating himself with the only woman he's ever lost his mind over, taking his revenge on her, claiming his baby and securing the succession. It's all simple and surefire. Until he sees her again…

THRONE OF JUDAR's three-book miniseries is my debut for the Desire line, where I felt at home at once, creating irresistible, larger-than-life heroes who meet their destinies in committed, passionate heroines during tempestuous journeys filled with pleasures and heartaches, until they reach their indisputably earned and gloriously satisfying happy endings.

Look out for Shehab's story in *The Desert Lord's Bride* in July 2008, then Kamal's in *The Desert King* in September 2008.

I would love to hear from you, so please contact me at www.oliviagates.com.

Olivia

THE
DESERT
LORD'S
BABY

OLIVIA GATES

Published by Silhouette Books

America's Publisher of Contemporary Romance

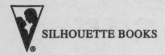

SILHOUETTE BOOKS

ISBN-13: 978-0-373-76872-1
ISBN-10:   0-373-76872-9

THE DESERT LORD'S BABY

Visit Silhouette Books at www.eHarlequin.com

Printed in U.S.A.

Books by Olivia Gates

Silhouette Desire

The Desert Lord's Baby #1872

Silhouette Bombshell

†*Strong Medicine* #63
†*Radical Cure* #80

*Throne of Judar
†Dr. Calista St. James stories

OLIVIA GATES

has always pursued creative passions—painting, singing and many handicrafts. She still does, but only one of her passions grew gratifying enough, consuming enough, to become an ongoing career. Writing.

She is most fulfilled when she is creating worlds and conflicts for her characters, then exploring and untangling them bit by bit, sharing her protagonists' every heart-wrenching heartache and hope, their every heart-pounding doubt and trial, until she leads them to an indisputably earned and gloriously satisfying happy ending.

When she's not writing, she is a doctor, a wife to her own alpha male and a mother to one brilliant girl and one demanding angora cat. Visit Olivia at www.oliviagates.com.

To an incredible lady, my editor Natashya Wilson,
for her belief in me, her constant encouragement
and spot-on guidance.

And to Desire's wonderful senior editor,
Melissa Jeglinski, for opening up a
fantastic new path for me.

Prologue

"Do you know what it felt like, being trapped for two days in those hellish negotiations, away from you?"

Farooq's voice swept over Carmen, dark and fathomless like the night sky she was staring into, the exotic accent turning it into a potent weapon, an irresistible spell.

She'd felt him the moment he'd entered the penthouse. The skyscraper. Long before that. Probably the moment he'd stepped out of the closed negotiations that had taken him away from her every day for the past six weeks. The nights had been all hers. All theirs. Madness and magic's.

She'd thought she'd braced herself, was ready for her first exposure to him after forty-eight hours of deprivation.

After she'd found out something that had changed her life forever.

She wasn't ready. His approach felt like that of a hurricane. Her teeth chattered with the convulsion of emotions ripping through her. How she *loved* him.

It had happened so fast, so totally. When she'd thought she stopped believing in love, wasn't even equipped to feel lust. Then, everything inside her had shuddered with the first sight of him, stumbled with the first hours in his company, crashed with the first night in his arms. She'd been hurtling deeper ever since.

She'd known that, when her time with him was up, she'd keep on plunging, hadn't cared what would happen then, had only been desperate to experience every minute afforded her of him.

Until today.

She gazed blindly through the floor-to-ceiling reinforced glass overlooking Manhattan, which sparkled beyond the sprawling darkness of Central Park. Each quiet step of now-bare feet on the luxurious carpet echoed inside her, along with the hiss of cashmere sliding off silk, then silk off living velvet steel, his masterpiece body slowly revealed, not in reflection, but in her memory, where his every nuance was etched in obsessive detail.

She still couldn't turn to him. The scalpel edge she'd been balancing on began to slice into her, cutting slow and deep.

This would be their last night.

She wanted to cram a lifetime into it. Tear open every second and fill it with him, with them. She wanted to consume him, *needed* all his contradictions, patience and arrogance, tenderness and ferocity, all devastating, all at once.

"Wahashteeni, ya ghalyah." His croon dipped into the bass reaches of her torment. Hearing him say he missed her, the endearment he favored—precious, treasured—hit a chord of blind yearning inside her. Her breasts heaved, her nipples hardened to points of agony. She couldn't bear the crush of cotton over her inflamed skin, the chafing emptiness inside her. Then he made it far worse. "I shouldn't have stayed away no matter what. Now I'm almost afraid to touch you, afraid that when I do, it will take us to the very edge of survival."

He was half a breath away now, and inside her a tornado tore everything apart. She gasped for air. It screeched down her lungs, riding a scent of intoxication, the musk of tension, virility and desire. Of him. A phantom touch moved her cascade of burgundy hair to one shoulder, exposing her neck. He leaned a fraction closer…and breathed. Inhaled her. Drew her whole into him.

Then his hands moved over her, hovering an inch away, creating a field of sensual friction. He brought his lips to her ear and his soft rumble hit her with the force of a clap of thunder. "I couldn't even call you, knew I'd lose every ground I'd won if I heard your voice, felt your desire. I would have dropped everything and come to you."

And she knew. She couldn't take even tonight with him.

If she did, she'd stay. And in six more weeks, he'd know.

He'd know she was pregnant.

And she couldn't let him know.

She'd promised him it was safe to make love without protection. And it hadn't been. He'd see her as a liar, a cheat. He'd be incensed. Or worse. Far worse.

He might have behaved magnificently with her, but she had no illusions about what she was to him. She was a diversion to let off steam during negotiations that taxed his soul and psyche. After that first night together, his offer had been clear. Be his lover during his three-month world tour to broker peace and relief. She was certain he intended to end their arrangement with all the largesse of the prince that he was, probably with an ultragenerous settlement. A settlement she would never have accepted.

But fate had given her something far more precious than anything he could have offered her, the ultimate gift…

She shuddered. She'd been so lost in misery, she'd left it too late to move away. Now he took her, wrapped her in his cabled arms, her back to his chest, her head in the curve of his neck as his towering body encompassed her, sending her reeling with wave after wave of such craving, she almost risked everything for one more taste of heaven in his arms. Almost.

She lurched out of his tightening embrace, tottering, trying to pretend it was a natural move, and croaked a distraction, "Did you manage to propose your relief projects without the Ashgoonian prime minister screaming that your monarchy has some nerve, criticizing his 'democracy's' internal affairs?"

It took him a moment to answer. A moment during which he tried to pull her back into his arms. A look of incomprehension stained his overpowering beauty when she evaded him again.

Then he seemed to dismiss her action as nothing to analyze, shrugged his Olympian shoulders. "He did better than that. He gave me unconditional access into Ashgoonian territory for a hundred-mile zone across the borders with Damhoor."

A surge of pleasure and pride in his extraordinary achievement, something the UN itself hadn't been able to manage, overtook her, momentarily suppressing her misery. "Oh, Farooq, that's incredible. You're going to save so many lives."

His sensuous lips twisted. "Let's not count our saved lives before they're saved, Carmen. In diplomacy I project only worst-case scenarios. But enough of that. I'm not Prince Aal Masood now. I'm the man who has untold pleasures in store for the woman who's his most magnificent gift for his life's best birthday."

His birthday. She'd found out only yesterday, and it had been during her shopping trip for supplies to make the man who had multitudes of everything a handmade gift that she'd collapsed, ended up in hospital and found out that what she'd thought impossible had happened. Farooq's baby was growing inside her.

He reached for her again. This time when she dodged him his arms fell to his sides and bewilderment flashed over his sculpted face. Then comprehension dawned in the honeyed depths of his eyes.

He exhaled. "It's that time of month at last?"

He thought she was having her period? God, how ironic. She grabbed at the excuse, nodded.

He sighed again. "It has been longer than expected coming, hasn't it?" He didn't even know how long it had been. And why should he? He wasn't counting the moments with her, counting down to the moment their time together came to an end. A wicked gleam suddenly entered his hypnotic eyes. "It'll never stop stunning me, how delightfully wanton you are at times only to squirm with shyness at others." She looked away from his teasing. A finger under her chin dragged her aching gaze back to his. "I may be burning to possess you, *ya ghalyah,* but I'll take equal pleasure in comforting you. You look so tired, so pale." He took her arm, pulled her toward the gigantic, circular bed draped in midnight blue silk. "Are you in any pain? I'll summon my physicians."

She shook her head, faltered. "I'm just…cramping a bit."

His smile was all indulgence. "Then I'll give you a massage. And under my hands, rubbed down with my kingdom's magical oils, all your aches and discomforts will dissolve."

The images he provoked speared through her loins, his thoughtfulness through her head and heart. She lurched away. *"No."*

The rugged majesty of his face stiffened with confusion. He approached her again, his hands spreading in solicitude that became bafflement, then frustration when she jumped out of reach again.

He finally rasped, "What's wrong?"

She had to do it now. Before she weakened. Before she succumbed. She blurted it out. "I'm going back home."

He stared at her, all expression frozen on his face. At last he inhaled.

"Again I ask, what's wrong?" His voice was measured now, careful, as if he were talking to a frightened mare.

"Nothing's wrong. I just want to go back to L.A."

Puzzlement and watchfulness still hovered in his eyes as he persisted. "And the reason is?"

Her gaze wavered, her lungs closed. She hadn't thought for

a second that his response to her declaration would be anything beyond a sigh and a shrug, before he moved on to the next conquest. His unexpected probing cornered her, made her blurt out the first thing that came to her. "I thought I was free to go whenever I wanted."

Imperiousness, something she knew was innate in him but which he'd never subjected her to, blazed in his eyes. "You're not. Not without justification for your abrupt demand."

Floundering, she said, "It's a *decision.* And it's not abrupt. I've been meaning to tell you for some time."

Harshness crept into his eyes, into his voice when he drawled, "Oh, yes? Were your cries for more forty-eight hours ago part of telling me you wanted to cut our time together short?"

She turned away. She'd collapse where she stood if she tried to hold his gaze one more second. He didn't let her get far, his hands clamping her shoulders, his lips feathering along her neck.

"Enough of this, Carmen." His groan jolted more longing and misery through her. "Whatever *this* is. If you're angry with me for some—"

She jerked out of his hands, rasped, "I'm not."

His jaw muscles worked. "There must be something. You can't just want to leave. I won't let you—"

And she cried out, the shrillness of panic creeping into her voice. "I'm not *asking* you if I can leave, I'm *informing* you."

His face became implacable. "You're going nowhere until you tell me the truth. If you're in any trouble—"

"I'm *not.*" God. She'd underestimated his sense of entitlement. She'd forgotten he was more than the man she loved with everything in her. He was a prince of unlimited power. He expected, and always got, his way. He'd probe and press until she broke down, gave him what he asked for. And she *couldn't.*

One way out flashed inside her mind. Desperate. Dangerous. She could think of nothing else.

Suppressing tremors of anguish and anxiety, she murmured, "Contrary to what you're used to in your native Judar where your word is law, this is a free country, your highness. A woman has the same rights as a man here to take her pleasure where she pleases, and change her mind when she pleases."

He flinched as if she'd slapped him. "And you've changed yours? When you can barely stand with wanting me?"

She felt the twitches of loss of control seizing her. God. She'd made her life's worst mistake coming back here, being so weak she'd needed to see him one last time. She should have just disappeared.

Feeling crazed with desperation, she taunted, "That is what you'd like to think, isn't it?"

He stared at her, his eyes deadening.

When he finally spoke, he sounded smooth, tranquil. "How about we drop the charade? I have nothing but games everywhere in my life. But in my bedroom I allow only sexual ones. You think the remaining six weeks should carry a more substantial price tag than sharing my bed and privileges? How remiss of me. I should have put an offer you can appreciate on the table. So if you have demands…" He suddenly yanked her to him, bent her over a potent arm, his other hand pressing her hips to his, his erection grinding against her long-molten core, the refined man she'd known receding fast. "*Make* them. I'll meet them, whatever they are."

Her heart crumpled.

Oh God. This had gotten uglier than anything she could have imagined. He thought she was bargaining with the unstoppable desire that had raged between them from the first glance. Though his repugnance was total, he seemed willing to pay anything for more of her.

She tore herself out of his arms. She had to end this. *Now.*

Only the ugliest lie would do.

Feeling the resignation of a death sentence settling over her, it flowed from her in a lifeless voice. "I thought I owed you the courtesy of not disappearing without saying goodbye. But it seems I should have spared myself the unpleasantness, should have known you'd react with the barbarism of your culture and the conceit of your inherited status. You may be good in bed, Farooq, but so are a hundred other men. I like variety, and I always leave when my lovers start to bore me. I thought it best to go before I was sick of you. I didn't want to spell it out, but it's clear I shouldn't have bothered with civility."

Before she collapsed at his feet in a weeping mess, she staggered around him, snatched up her handbag, images of a baby who looked like him fueling her march out of his bedroom, out of his world.

But the image that would remain imprinted on her retinas for the rest of her life was of his face. The face of the hostile stranger she'd managed to turn him into in mere minutes.

The hostile stranger she'd never see again.

One

"Bagha...bagha..."

Carmen paused in the middle of hanging the nursery's new curtains. She looked down at Mennah, listened to her chirping her latest "word," her heart in a state of expansion.

She'd gotten used to feeling her heart filling her whole chest, her whole being, since she'd given birth to her daughter.

She'd demanded Mennah the moment she'd come out of her womb, disregarding the doctor's grumbling that he had to close said womb first. He'd succumbed, though, had placed the smeared, nine-pound miracle on Carmen's bosom. And for long moments, as she'd first touched her baby, felt her precious weight, her flesh and heat and reality, Carmen had been afraid she wouldn't survive the explosion of emotions raging through her.

She'd searched for the right name long and hard. She'd found the perfect one, what this baby was, in her father's mother tongue. Mennah. Her gift from God.

Now her gift was latching chubby fingers onto her play-pen's railings, hauling herself up to a standing position. She then tried to stand unsupported and landed on her diaper-padded bottom with a cry of chagrin-mixed glee, tearing a laugh from Carmen's depths.

"Oh, Mennah, darling, you're in such a hurry."

And she was. At only nine months, she'd been sitting un-supported for almost three, crawling for almost two and was now clearly on her way to overtaking another milestone.

Carmen slotted the last hook, climbed down the ladder and headed to the playpen. Her sunny angel grinned at her, good nature brimming from golden eyes, displaying her newly acquired set of teeth, her dimples flashing in the perfection of her cherubic face. A surge of emotions clogged Carmen's throat, rising to her eyes.

Could she have been so blessed?

Mennah held up her arms. Carmen obliged at once, bent and cradled the robust little body that was her reason for living. Mennah mashed her face into her mother's neck, and Carmen's arms convulsed around her. It was a good thing Mennah loved fierce hugs. Carmen bore down on the flare of love, rocked Mennah in her arms, one hand luxuriating in the raven silk of her locks. Hmm, the bald patch from before Mennah started rolling around was totally gone.

Suddenly Mennah pushed away, looked up expectantly. "Bagha bagha."

Carmen tickled her nose. "Yes, darling, you're trying to tell me something and your mommy is so dense she hasn't figured it out yet. But that's a new word. Give me a day and I'll figure it out. Say—could it be you're telling me you're hungry? It has been a couple of hours since you've eaten." Carmen started to undo her shirt only for Mennah to slap her hands on top of Carmen's, squealing, part playful, part admonish-ing. Carmen sighed. "No mommy-produced sustenance?"

Mennah giggled. Carmen sighed again. She'd been hoping

to prolong nursing. But this was another area where Mennah was in a hurry. She'd been refusing to nurse more and more ever since she'd been introduced to solid foods, decreasing Carmen's milk flow. This was the second day with no nursing at all. During that time Mennah had even given her grief about eating previously much-loved foods. And Carmen could guess why.

"I shouldn't have given you a taste of my filet mignon, darling. Seems you share more than your looks with your father. He, too, is a big panther who relishes red meat—"

Carmen stopped. Mennah was looking up at her with such absorption, as if she was memorizing everything her mother said.

Carmen had been indulging in the heartbreaking pleasure of constantly talking to her about her father. Maybe she should resist giving in to the urge. There was no way Mennah understood now, but maybe before Carmen realized, she would. And she didn't want to explain her father's absence for years. Not that she'd ever have enough time to come up with an adequate explanation.

Exhaling, shaking off a resurgence of the despondency that had suffocated her all through her pregnancy, she walked out of the nursery, headed to their open plan, sunlit kitchen.

She secured Mennah in her high chair, dropped a kiss on top of her glossy head. "One bagha bagha coming up."

She placed plastic toys in front of Mennah, set the iPod to a slow rock collection and started preparing the dish that had converted her baby to gourmet cuisine. Amidst singing along with her favorite songs and Mennah's accompanying shrieks of enthusiasm, she stopped periodically to gather the toys with which Mennah gleefully tested gravity, giving them back to her so she'd restart her experiments over and over again.

She was finishing the mushroom sauce when she noticed it had been a couple of minutes since she'd fetched for Mennah, since her daughter's squeals had disharmonized with her singing.

She turned around and her heart overflowed with another gush of love. Mennah was out like a light on the high chair's tray.

She always did fall asleep without warning. But she couldn't have been hungry after all, if she could fall asleep among all those mouthwatering aromas.

Sighing, eyeing the meal that had to be served hot to be good, Carmen turned off the music, unbuckled Mennah from her seat then went to put her down in her crib.

The singing had stopped.

The crashing of Farooq's heart hadn't.

And it wasn't only his heart that manifested his upheaval. Every muscle in his body was clenched, every nerve discharging.

He'd been standing there for what felt like a day, listening to the sounds coming from inside. Wistful love songs accompanied by the gleeful noises of an infant. And the overpowering melody of a siren.

He'd willed himself over and over to ring the bell. Better still, to break down the door.

He'd just stood there, his ear almost to the door to catch every decibel of a slice of life of the tiny family that lived inside, his hands caressing the door as if it were them.

He felt as if he'd disintegrate with an emotion so fierce he had no name for it, no experience and no way to deal with it.

It had to be rage. An unknown level that made what he'd felt when Carmen had told him she was leaving pale in comparison. It dwarfed what he'd felt when he'd pursued her, bent on erasing the ugliness, the madness of that confrontation, on bringing back his Carmen and the perfection they'd shared, only for more betrayal to tear at him when he'd seen her getting into his cousin Tareq's car. It even eclipsed what he'd felt when he'd confronted Tareq and discovered why she'd really left.

His cousin and arch nemesis had confessed that he'd sent

Carmen to seduce Farooq, to get pregnant and create a scandal large enough to stop Farooq's rise to the succession. Tareq had snickered that their uncle's latest decree had thrown a sabot in the cogs of his treachery, turning a pregnancy into an asset, not a liability, forcing him to order Carmen to leave, going back to the drawing board to think of something else to eliminate Farooq from the running.

It had all made sense to Farooq then. From the moment he'd seen her to the moment she'd walked out on him.

Or he'd thought it had.

It had been only hours ago that he'd learned the full truth. Another tidal wave of emotion crashed over him.

Ya Ullah—he'd never struggled for control, had never even contemplated its loss. He'd been born in control, of himself before others. His urges and desires were his to command, never the other way around. Then there was Carmen.

He'd lost control with his first sight of her, had lost his discretion while drowning in her pleasures, had almost lost his restraint upon her desertion.

Now he was a hairsbreadth from losing his reason.

And it was her doing yet again.

He leaned his forehead on the door, forced inhalations into his spastic lungs, order into his frenzied thoughts, willing the blinding seizure to pass.

It took minutes and the nosiness of two neighbors to bring him down. He regained at least enough control to settle a semblance of composure over the chaos, smothering it. Enough to make him reach a resolution.

He'd never let her affect him that deeply again. Ever.

He'd go in, take what he wanted. As he always did.

He straightened, set his teeth with great precision and almost drove his finger through her doorbell.

Carmen jerked up from watching Mennah sleep. The bell! Though it almost never rang, she'd been waiting for her super to come fix the short-circuit in the laundry room. He'd said within the next two days. *Four* days ago.

But it was the way the bell rang that had made her jump. It had almost…bellowed, for lack of a better description. Maybe it was about to give, too, and that sound was its dying throes?

Sighing, she checked Mennah's monitor and the wireless receiver clipped to her jeans' waist. On her way to the door, she smoothed her hands over her hair but gave up in midmotion with a huff. A disheveled greeter was what her super got for coming unannounced, catching a single mother with a dozen chores behind her and a shower still in her future.

Fixing a smile on her lips, intending her greeting to be thanks for his arrival if no thanks for his delay, she opened the door.

Her heart didn't stop immediately.

It went on with its rhythm for a moment, the kind that simulated hours, before it lost the blood it needed to keep on pumping. The blood now shooting to her head, pooling in her legs. Then it stopped.

And everything else hurtled, screeched, into consciousness.

Denial, dread, desperation.

She'd changed her career to work from home, had relocated to the other side of the continent, had still remained scared that he'd find her. But he hadn't, and eventually she'd believed he hadn't tried, or hadn't been able to.

But he *had* found her. Was on her doorstep. *Farooq.*

Filling her doorway. Blocking out existence.

She found herself slumped against the door, her fingers almost breaking off with the force with which they clutched it. Some instinct must have remained functioning, saving her from crashing to the ground. Some auxiliary power must be fueling her continued grip on consciousness.

"Save it."

That was all he said as he pushed past her, walking into her apartment as if he owned it. And his voice…

This wasn't the voice etched in her memory. The voice that

echoed in every moment's silence, haunting her, whispering seduction, rumbling arousal, roaring completion, always charged with emotion. *This* voice contained as much life as a voice simulation program.

God, what was he doing here?

No. She didn't care what he was doing here. She didn't care that her insides were crumbling under the avalanche of emotion the sight of him had triggered.

She had to get rid of him. *Fast.*

She had to regain control first, of her coherence, to think of something to say, of her volition, to be able to say it.

She leaned against the door she didn't remember closing, feeling as if the least tremor would shatter the tension keeping her upright. She watched his powerful strides take him into the formal living room, felt him shrinking it, converging all light on him like a spotlight in the dark.

And even through her shock and panic, everything inside her devoured each line of his juggernaut's body, even bigger and taller than she remembered, the sculpted suit worshipping it from the daunting breadth of shoulders, to the sparseness of waist and hips, to the formidable power of thighs and endless legs.

Memory was a sadistic master, lashing open festering wounds with images and sensations, of those shoulders dominating her, those hips thrusting her to a frenzy, those thighs and legs encompassing her in the aftermath of madness.

She tore her gaze and memories away, choking on longing. Then he turned, and everything in her piled up with the brunt of his beauty, the rawness of her still-burning love.

His heavy-lidded gaze documented her reaction before he raised both eyebrows, a movement rich in nonchalance and imperiousness. "Finished with your latest act, or shall I wait until you've delivered the full performance?"

It wasn't only his voice that was different. This wasn't the Farooq she remembered. This wasn't even the hostile stranger she'd walked out on. That man had been seething with harshness, with emotion. *This* man was even more forbidding, as he eyed her with the clinical coldness of a scientist dealing with inanimate matter.

His lips pursed as if he were assessing a defective product. He finally gave a slight shake of his awesome head, lips twisting on his unfavorable verdict. "As an unbiased viewer, I must tell you, your acting abilities are slipping. Exaggeration is not your friend."

Before she could even process his dispassionate comment, let alone find words to answer it, he relieved her of his focus, cast his gaze around her space.

She could see his connoisseur's mind adding up the worth of every square foot, every piece of furniture, brush stroke and decorative article and felt defensive. Though she'd made this place chic and cheery, it could well be derelict compared to the opulence he was used to. Which was a stupid thing to feel and think.

She had to make him leave. Now. Before Mennah woke up. Before he saw the childproofing she'd begun installing.

He finally returned those empty eyes to hers as he walked back toward her. She watched him cross the distance between them with the fatalism of someone about to be hit by a train.

"It cost a bundle, this place," he murmured. "I would have wondered how you afforded it. If I didn't already know."

She almost blurted out "What do you mean by that?"

She didn't. She couldn't locate her voice. Her heart had long invaded her throat. She could barely breathe enough to keep from passing out. And his indifference and disparagement were encasing her in frost, hurrying her descent. Everything was taking on a surreal tinge. She began to hope this was a scenario out of her Farooq-starved imagination.

Then he was within touching distance. And she had to prove to herself he was—or wasn't—really here.

She reached out a trembling hand, half expecting her fingertips to encounter a mirage. Instead they feathered over black-silk-covered flesh, the layered sensations of softness and steel, heat and hardness. Her fingers pressed into him, shudders engulfing her, like an electrocution victim unable to break the deadly circuit.

And she saw it, in his eyes. A response, blasting away the ice, mushrooming like a nuclear cloud before the wave of annihilation followed. Before he clamped onto her intruding hand.

A moan punched out of her as he squeezed awareness from her flesh and bones. Then, with scary precision, he removed her hand from his chest, let it drop like a soiled tissue.

With his eyes empty again, he half turned, raising his head as if sniffing for an oncoming storm.

"Hmm…filet mignon with mushroom sauce?" He turned his eyes to her. They weren't back to impassivity at all, the harshness she'd seen in them that night in his penthouse polluting the amber. "Expecting a guest? Or is it a sponsor?" She gaped at him. His voice dipped into an abrasive bass. "I hope you've had enough of the shocked routine and will contribute to what started as a monologue and is now bordering on a soliloquy."

Contribute. He wanted her to contribute. She had exactly four words to contribute. The sum total of what was left of her mind.

"Why are you here?"

Something feral flashed in the depths of his wolflike eyes. "So, you deem to end the mute show. If only to put on the dumb one."

Each word was a lash on her rawness. "Please…*stop*."

He inclined his head, a predator at leisure, his prey cornered, with all the time in the world to torment it. "Stop what? Critiquing your below par performance? You have only yourself to blame for that. It seems you haven't been honing your craft of late."

"Please…I don't understand."

"More acts, Carmen? Don't you know the key to a successful acting career, especially an offstage one, is sticking with your strengths? My advice: never try the particular roles you just churned up for my benefit again. They neither suit nor work."

"For God's sake, stop talking in riddles. *Why are you here?*"

He raised an eyebrow. "Intent on dramatizing to the end, aren't you? Or are you just intent on testing the limits of my patience? The reason I'm here is self-evident."

She shook her head. "Not to me. So please, drop *your* act and just say what you came here to say, and then—*please*—leave me alone."

He seemed to expand like a thundercloud about to hurtle down destruction, a beam of the day's dying sun striking a solar flare of rage in the gold of his eyes.

"I once told you that I have my fill of games. I thought you had enough intelligence not to join the would-be manipulators who swarm around me. At least not to try the same trick twice. Evidently I've overestimated your IQ. This will be the last time I take part in one of *your* games, so savor it while you can. Try another at your peril." He inclined his head at her, sent her heart slamming in her chest. "You want me to pretend I don't know that you know why I'm here? *Zain.* Fine." He gave a pause laden with the irony of someone about to deliver something redundant, the disgust of being forced to play an offensive game of make-believe.

Then he drawled, smooth and sharp as a razor, "I am here for my daughter."

Two

Farooq's words shot through Carmen, pulverizing the framework holding her heart in place. Yet something kept her on her feet and conscious. Probably hope that she was hallucinating. "W-what did you say?"

He exhaled, the icy armor not back in place, the underlying volcano seething through the cracks. "Spare me further theatrics. You had my daughter. You *have* my daughter. I am here for her."

He knows about Mennah.

How could he know about her?

He somehow did, had said…said…

I am here for my daughter.

What did that mean? Here for her…how? It couldn't mean what it sounded like. It couldn't mean he…he…

He wanted to take Mennah away from her.

The ground softened. An abyss yawned beneath, pulled at her…

But no. *No.* Not even he could take a baby away from her mother. This wasn't Judar, where he was the law. This was America.

But how did he find out? Had he had her investigated, found out she'd had a baby, done the math and come to the conclusion Mennah might be his? Why would he want her even if he realized she was? He couldn't consider her anything but a disastrous mistake.

That first night he'd had no protection, and even in the inferno of arousal, he would have stopped if she hadn't assured him she was safe. She'd been certain she was. She'd had a dozen reports from as many specialists declaring her infertile.

He'd told her in blatant detail how he wanted to invade her, feel his flesh inside hers without barriers, to pour himself inside her. It had sent her up in flames in his arms…

Stop. *Stop.* She couldn't let those memories assault her now. He hadn't been risking repercussions, had believed her assurances. That was why she'd known his reaction would be violent if he found out about her pregnancy. He would have looked upon it as an ultimate breach of the trust he didn't give easily. Most important, she couldn't have projected how damaging it would be to him, a prince in line to the throne of one of the world's most conservative and richest oil states, to have an illegitimate child.

Suddenly her heart nearly fired out of her ribs.

Could he be here to make sure Mennah disappeared, so she'd never compromise his position?

Out of her mind with dread, she asked, "What makes you even think my daughter can be yours?"

His answering stare was long and pitiless, lava coursing beneath the dark, hard surface.

Then he dipped one hand inside his jacket, as if he were extracting a gun.

Next moment she wished he had pulled one out, had shot her straight through the heart with it.

He pulled out a photo instead. Of Mennah.

A photo of Mennah sitting in strange surroundings. Holding an unfamiliar toy. Wearing unknown clothes. Mennah was laughing at the camera, secure, pleased, knowing how to please.

Mennah was only like that around her.

In the few times she'd seen other people, she'd clung to Carmen, fearful, tearful. If someone had managed to get her alone…

Was she losing her mind? How could she be wondering that?

She'd *never* left Mennah alone, except when she was sound asleep in her crib, like now. She'd diverted her career to work from home so she could be with her daughter at all times.

How had he gotten his hands on Mennah?

"I—I've never left Mennah. When—how did you get the chance to—to—"

"I didn't." His voice slashed across her babbling. "This isn't a photo of your…of *my* daughter. This is a photo of my sister, Jala, at Mennah's age. Mennah is also my feminine replica at that age. That Mennah is mine is indisputable. So let's drop the hysterics and get to the point of all this."

"Wh-what is that?"

"That I'll never forgive you for keeping her from me."

Farooq's gaze clung to Carmen as she flinched as if at the lash of a whip, his fascination beyond his control.

But that was an improvement on what had happened when she'd opened her door with that smile ready on her lips. Everything had stilled then. Thought, heartbeats. Time itself had seemed to stop.

Then it had hit a screeching reverse, catapulting him to the moment he'd first laid eyes on her in that conference hall a year and a half ago.

As a tycoon and a prince, he had the world's most spectacular beauties flaunting their assets and practicing seduction for his benefit. His attention had to be worked for extensively, was held with utmost effort for periods never surpassing days.

Then *she'd* come forward, hesitant, prim, and his focus had been captured and his lust aroused, effortlessly. Absolutely. A surge of something he'd never entertained feeling—possessiveness—had followed.

He'd wanted to banish every male around, shield her from their eyes and thoughts. Not that she'd been inviting attention. No doubt as part of her plan to stand out.

Apart from her aloofness, she'd been smothered in a navy skirt suit from neck to mid-calf, when all the women around her had worn skirts riding up their thighs and blouses opened on deep cleavages.

Her closed expression and concealing clothes had made him more eager to tear through them. He'd seen himself stripping her of that guarded look, those offending coverings, arranging her on that conference table, spreading her for his pleasure and hers, her reserve melting as she begged for his pleasuring, writhed for his domination…

It must have been the response she'd counted on. That the mystique of her reticence in manner and dress would rouse the hunter lying dormant inside him. And it had worked. Spectacularly.

For the first time ever, he'd been fazed, couldn't account for his violent response. Unlike many men of his culture, he didn't prefer fair-skinned, light-eyed women, certainly never redheads.

But she'd approached him like a wary gazelle, her equal attraction and alarm blazing in those heaven-colored eyes, had put that supple hand in his and everything about her had become everything he craved. Her face and body had become the sum total of his fantasies, every feature and line the source of his hunger, the fuel for his pleasure.

He would have done anything to have her in his bed. And when by the end of the night he'd had her there, he couldn't let it end, had offered what he'd never offered any woman. Three months. In the private space he never let anyone breach. With every minute, he'd wanted her for longer. He'd even entertained forever.

Then she'd walked out.

Ever since, he'd been trying to wipe her taste from his mouth, the memory of her from his psyche, to reacquire a taste for other brands of beauty, build tolerance for another's touch.

After each dismal failure he'd damned her, damned his addiction more. And here he was, renewing his exposure.

She'd opened the door, and it had been as if everything he'd learned since she'd revealed her true face had been erased, and she was again the woman he'd run back to that night, intending to offer forever.

It had taken her spectacular reaction to seeing him to jog him out of his amnesic haze. To fire his memory of when she'd done the unprecedented. The unimaginable. Thrown his desire back in his face. Been the one to walk out.

He'd pretended interest in his surroundings to tear his senses away, only for everything about her new home to send his fury cresting, proof of her crimes against him.

Had this place been stripped of even a coat of paint, it would still cost a fortune, with its location in an elite building in an upmarket neighborhood of one of the most expensive cities in the world, New York. The fortune she'd made being Tareq's mole.

Tareq had planted her in his life at the perfect time. During his taxing world tour, as he'd fought for his goals on all fronts, amidst Tareq's escalating efforts to discredit him.

He'd thought her a godsend. Instead she'd been sent by a devil. A devil whose evil had backfired.

With Farooq's father dead—of a broken heart, Farooq was convinced, just a year after Farooq's mother had died from a long illness—Tareq had thought that, as the king's oldest nephew, he'd succeed Farooq's father as crown prince.

Tareq's own father had died of a heart attack when they were all quite young, leaving Tareq his only heir and the oldest of the royal cousins.

But, knowing that Tareq favored certain unkingly, depraved activities, their uncle the king had at first said he'd reserve the crown prince title for his own son. A son he could only have if he took a second wife. When he couldn't bring himself to take another wife, he'd then said he'd name his heir according to merit, not age, with the implication clear to all that he meant Farooq and would soon officially name him crown prince. Tareq had then launched into non-stop plotting to overrule the king's decree.

During Farooq's tour, Tareq had suddenly started talking as if he'd secured the succession, bragging that he'd be the first king who never married. Farooq guessed he'd said that to gain the support of the enemies of the royal house of Aal Masood by intimating that they would therefore get a turn to rule after him. He now realized that Tareq had also thought his plot with Carmen had been about to bear fruit, creating an illegitimate, half-western heir for Farooq and eliminating him from favor.

But Tareq's assertions had only given the king ammunition to overcome the reluctance of the members of the Tribune of Elders—the king's council—who had resisted bypassing Tareq for Farooq. With Tareq adding contempt for the Aal Masoods' future to his depravities, the king knew that all Farooq needed to do to drive the last nail in Tareq's coffin was to overcome his own reluctance to marry. Didn't he have a woman he'd consider marrying? his uncle had asked.

Farooq hadn't even hesitated. He had a woman. Carmen.

And his king had issued the decree. The heir who married and produced the first child would succeed to the throne.

And Tareq had ordered Carmen to leave the very next day.

During their confrontation, Tareq had thanked his lucky stars that Carmen hadn't conceived, casting aspersions on Farooq's virility and fertility. Sixteen hours ago, Farooq had realized she'd left because she *had* conceived, the child that would have snuffed her employer's dying hopes.

She couldn't have known what she'd lost when she'd run out on him. But he still didn't know why she hadn't stayed to use the child as a bargaining chip, had taken Tareq's offer instead. Even if she'd shown Farooq the face of a woman he could never marry, he'd been in addiction's merciless grip, would have given her light years beyond what she had now.

Had she thought he'd sate himself, wreak vengeance on her then discard her with nothing? Or did her subservience to Tareq mix greed with fear? Or even lust…?

His thoughts boiled in an uproar of revulsion.

Thinking of her in Tareq's filthy arms, succumbing to his sadism and perversions… Bile rose up to his throat.

But the sick image of her as his cousin's tool and whore, and her own words as she'd left him, clashed with everything radiating from her now….

No. He'd never believe anything he sensed about her again. He could still barely believe how totally he'd been taken in, how seamlessly she'd acted her part. It had been a virtuoso performance, the guilelessness, the spontaneity, the unbridled responses, the perpetual hunger, the total pleasure in him, in and out of bed.

But all that faking had borne something real. A daughter. And he'd missed so much. The miracle of her birth and every precious moment of the first nine months of her life.

And if it had been up to Carmen, he would have never found out about her. She would have grown up fatherless.

But among all Carmen's crimes, what most enraged him had been that *touch*.

She'd touched him as if to ascertain he was really there. And that touch had almost made him drag her to the floor, tear her out of her clothes and bury himself inside her.

Now he relished repaying her for shredding his control yet again, seeing her with her composure shattered.

Oh, yes. *That* was real. She must be frantic, thinking her cash cow had run dry. Now that Farooq had learned of Mennah's existence, Tareq would stop paying for her luxurious lifestyle.

Seething with colliding emotions, he inclined his head at her. "Nothing to say, I see. That's very wise of you."

She gulped. "H-how did you find out?"

He wouldn't have. Ever. If he'd stuck to his oath never to seek her out. But instead of fading away, her memory had burned hotter each day, and the need for closure had almost driven him mad.

It had taken months, even with the endless resources at his fingertips, to find her. His best people had finally gotten him the basics—an address, a resume…and a photograph. Of Carmen and a baby. A baby recognizable on sight as his.

That photograph now burned a rectangle its size over his heart, though he'd chosen to show Carmen Jala's photo instead, to cut things short. He'd expected her to contest his paternity.

Pursing his lips, he pushed past her. "I find out anything I want. Now, I'll see my daughter."

"No." She grabbed him, aborting his stride toward the hall leading to the bedrooms. Her touch, though frantic, still sent a bolt of arousal through him. He added his unwilling response to her transgressions, looked down at her hands in disgust, at her, at himself. She removed them, took a step backward. "She's sleeping."

"So? Fathers walk in on their sleeping daughters all the time. You've taken nine months of my daughter's life away from me. I'm not letting you take one more minute."

She jumped into his path again, her color dangerous, her chest heaving. "I'll let you see her only if—if you promise—"

He slashed his hand, cutting off her wobbling words. "Nobody *lets* me do anything, let alone you. I do what I see fit. And everyone obeys."

He took another step and she threw herself at him, imprinting him with her lushness. His body roared even through the fury.

He gritted his teeth. "Get out of my way, Carmen. You're not coming between me and my flesh and blood again."

She clung, gasped, "I didn't—"

"You didn't?" He held her away with fingers that even now luxuriated in the feel of her resilient flesh, longed to run all over her. "What else do you call what you did?"

A sob rattled deep inside her, made him want to clamp his lips on hers, plunge inside her fragrant warmth, plunder her until he'd extracted it, and her perfidious soul with it. Instead he relinquished his hold on her, unhooked her frantic fingers from his flesh with utmost control, put her away. She stumbled back, ended up plastered to the hall entrance, her eyes, those luminous pieces of his kingdom's summer skies, welling with terrible emotions. Emotions he knew she didn't have.

His anger spiked. "What do you call keeping her a secret? Or trying to deny my paternity now?"

"Please, stop." She spread her arms over the entry when he moved, intending to brush her aside. "I did it because I know that, in your culture, illegitimacy remains your deepest entrenched stigma and that to a prince like you, having a lover bear you an illegitimate child would be an irreparable scandal..."

He looked down into her eyes. *Ya Ullah,* how could they be so guileless? So potent? How could lies be so undetectable?

"So you are an expert on my culture and my status?" he grated. "And you left, and left me in the dark that I'd fathered a daughter, to observe the demands of both?"

She nodded, shook her head, at a total loss. "Oh God, please..." She paused, then panted, "How could I have told you I was pregnant? When I told you it couldn't happen?"

He gave a shrug. "Just like any woman who gets pregnant after such protestations would have. That it just happened. I'm sure the statistical failure of contraceptive measures has come to the rescue of countless women in your position." Those ruby lips trembled on what he knew would be another ultra sincere-sounding protest. Before he closed them with his own, he plowed on, "And then I'm well aware of the facts of life, and if I'd wanted to be positive I didn't impregnate you, I would have handled protection myself, not left it up to you and your assurances of safety. But I didn't."

And how well he remembered why he hadn't.

That first night, by the end of their dinner, he'd been in agony. But he'd been willing, for the first time in his life, to wait for a woman. He'd wanted the perfection to continue, had wanted to give her time, give himself more of her, without the intimacies he'd been burning for. The unprecedented feelings of closeness and rapport, the sheer delight in everything about her had been incredible enough; he would have savored them without fulfillment of the carnal promise indefinitely. He'd resolved to end the night with a kiss and no more. Then she'd sabotaged his intentions, pulverized his expectations.

She'd offered herself with such a mixture of shyness, passion and resolve that he'd almost refused. She'd aroused in him what he'd never felt toward a female outside his family. Tenderness, protectiveness. She'd seemed in an agony of embarrassment at her demand, yet in the grips of a hunger she couldn't control. She'd tremulously told him she knew she'd be a one-night stand for him but she had to have it, would settle for any taste of him.

He'd had her in his quarters without realizing how, had too late remembered protection, had been loath to send for it. He'd told her he'd still pleasure her, and she could pleasure him, if she wanted. She'd clung to him, said she was safe, in every way.

He hadn't even questioned her honesty, his relief sweeping. He'd wanted her to be his first. The first woman he experienced to the fullness of intimacy, his flesh driving in hers, feeling the heat and moistness of her need for him, without barriers. The first woman he poured himself into. And all through the magical six weeks he'd done that, had each glorious time abandoned himself inside her in the throes of completion. And trust.

His lips twisted in disgust, at what even memories did to him. "I didn't," he repeated. "So whatever blame there is, I share it in equal measure. Not that the word *blame* applies anywhere in the conception of a child. Certainly not my child."

She crumpled against the entryway, as if from a blow, and hiccupped, "I—I had no way of knowing you could have felt this way. You didn't want me beyond those three months and I thought you couldn't possibly want the baby I accidentally got pregnant with…"

He growled a laugh. "Accidentally? Really? But no matter how or why you got pregnant, I don't care. I don't care how my daughter was conceived, I don't care who conceived her, not even if it's you. She's mine. And I want her."

Her reaction to that was spectacular.

Springing from the entryway, she advanced on him like a lioness ready to defend her cub to the death.

"No," she growled. There was no other way to describe it. She *growled.* "She's not yours. She's mine. *Mine.*"

He frowned. This felt too real.

But no more real than what *he* felt. He, too, felt like baring his fangs in demand of the daughter who'd been kept from him. His body bunched with the elemental instinct, its fire spitting through eyes slitting on fury and challenge.

"You want to fight me for her?" he snarled. "Do I need to tell you that nobody wins in any kind of battle with me, that your chances of winning anything against me are below non-existent?"

The contortion of horror and desperation that crumpled her expression did something similar behind his breastbone.

Ya Ullah, how did she *do* that?

She sagged back against the door as if the knowledge of his unstoppable power sank inside her, draining her of hers.

At last she rasped, "Why are you doing this?"

Could defeat have a sound? If it did, this must be it.

"I told you. I want my daughter." He paused, unsure what he wanted to say or do anymore. Her essence was seeping through him, dissolving his resolve, rearranging his thoughts, rewriting her character in his mind again. He ground his teeth against the weakening. "And I will have her."

And the eyes that had been brimming with tears gushed.

He'd seen her tears before. When he'd drawn out her torment before he'd ended it, shattering her with releases so fierce she'd wept with them. Now, seeing new tears pouring from eyes so crimsoned he feared they might seep blood at any moment, he could no longer dispute her state.

Whatever the reason behind her anguish, it was real, profound. She was more terrified, more desperate now than if she believed he intended to end her life.

He stared at her, an overwhelming need rising, to soothe away the pain he'd caused her. He curled his fists against the urge.

"Please…understand…I o-only hid my pregnancy b-because I was s-scared you'd make me terminate it!"

Her words detonated inside him, the belief that it was all an act erased in the blast. All he heard was the accusation, all he believed was that *she'd* believed it.

"You thought I would ask you to kill an unborn child? *My* unborn child? And you think you know anything about my culture or me? And when she was born, what did you fear? That I'd bury her alive like my land's barbarians of old?"

"No." Her cry was engulfed by shearing sobs. She still talked through them. "All I thought was you—you might fear her existence, might think her a threat to your honor, your status… And I wasn't risking it. I would do anything—*anything*—to keep her from harm."

"And you thought I'd harm her? You saw me fighting to bring relief to millions of children and thought I'd harm my own?"

B'Ellahi, what was he saying? He was playing the part she'd shoved him into with all the oblivious fervor of the past. He was answering her as if he believed concern for her baby and true fear of his reactions had been the reasons behind her disappearance.

"B'haggej'Jaheem—by Hell, I thought you'd come up with better than that. Or maybe you didn't give it much thought since you were sure this confrontation would never come to pass."

She shook her head, sending her tears splashing everywhere. A few fell on his hands, felt as if they'd burned him to the bone.

"But why do you want her?" And if he'd thought she'd given defeat sound, she now gave desperation tone and texture. "Don't Judarians value only male sons? What is a daughter to a prince like you who surely wants only heirs?"

"So, first you dare to imply that I might have gotten rid of her for being born at all, and now that I'd discard her for being born female."

She spread her hands in a helpless gesture, a lost gesture, beseeching his understanding, his mercy.

He had neither to give. "Enough of that."

She again threw herself in his path, but was shaking so hard she couldn't even cling. "I didn't dream you'd want her... please..."

He looked down at her, struggling with the need to slake the accumulation of hunger in that body that had deprived him of finding pleasure elsewhere. He'd been unable to contemplate marrying another after she'd walked out on him, even as a damage-control measure when Tareq had rushed out and married the first woman to accept him. Instead, Farooq had decided to expose Tareq's ineligibility to rise to the succession once and for all, had asked his king, who couldn't go back on the marriage-criteria decree, to stall everyone until he furnished irrefutable proof of Tareq's perversions and crimes.

He was close to gaining that proof, but now he'd found Carmen and Mennah—and they were the fastest route to securing the succession. Not that he would let Tareq go unpunished. Or Carmen, either. But he wouldn't touch her. Not yet.

Putting her away was harder than anything he'd ever had to do. Then he strode through the entrance she'd been guarding, went deeper into the apartment, felt her stumbling behind him, her tremors buzzing through his flesh, her sobs constricting his lungs.

He ignored the feelings, stopped before the door that he just knew had his daughter on the other side. Then he turned.

"Show me my daughter, Carmen."

He had no idea why he asked her permission when he never asked anyone's, gave her that consideration when she'd shown him none. Worst of all, he had no idea why he'd done it so…gently.

That was for his daughter, he told himself. He didn't want to enter her room, her life, with anger polluting those first magical moments. Children picked up on moods, deciphered tension between adults. And he wasn't poisoning her mood or introducing fear and anxiety in her life for any reason, was even willing to make peace with her mother, if only around her, for her sake.

"Stop crying. I won't have my daughter see me for the first time with her mother weeping beside me. She'd forever link me with your pain."

"A-and she'd be right…you're destroying me."

He grimaced his distaste at her exaggeration. "Cut the melodrama, Carmen. Or are you willing to risk scarring her impressionable psyche just to paint me black in her mind?"

"No, no…I'd never…never…" She almost fell at his feet, forced him to take her full weight, his hands around her rib cage, so close to the breasts that were now shuddering with emotion, that had once shuddered in his palms, beneath his chest in ecstasy. She raised rabid eyes to his and wailed, "Don't take my daughter away…I'd die without her."

Three

Farooq stared down at Carmen for a stunned moment.

He had heard about the power of tears before, had had them shed for his benefit on countless occasions, by both women and men. The only power they'd held over him was that of testing the limits of his goodwill. But *her* tears…

Ya Ullah, hada mostaheel—it was impossible the way they affected him, the way her outburst had.

She thought he intended to take her baby away.

It was only in this moment that he realized he'd stormed in here not knowing *what* he intended.

He'd gotten the intel sixteen hours ago, had been on his fastest jet within an hour, had spent the time on the nonstop transcontinental, transatlantic haul seething with realizations and convictions. Some of the latter *had* been of how an exploitative mother didn't deserve to keep her child.

He now realized those thoughts had colored the way he'd stated his intention of having his daughter, making it sound as if he'd snatch her away from Carmen.

He believed that drastic action should be reserved for women who were a danger to their offspring. But, couldn't he equate a mother who used her daughter to maintain a luxurious lifestyle with an alcoholic or a drug addict?

Rage shot to another zenith as he looked down into her drenched eyes. Then, to his further fury, her anguish fractured his grip on his convictions.

As their eyes meshed, all he could think of was that this was no act. This wasn't someone afraid for her income. This was someone who feared something far worse than death.

Could it be true? She'd conceived Mennah for an ulterior motive, but she now loved her? And that much?

He *could* take her—*his*—daughter from her as easily as taking a toy from an infant. Considering what she'd done to him, he should at least entertain retribution. The thought only scorched him with mortification.

She had to be some sort of witch.

But then, all he'd meant when he'd declared she couldn't fight him was that she couldn't deny him his right to his daughter. She'd taken his words to their worst possible conclusion. That was in keeping with the fear she claimed had driven her to run away. So could he believe that had really been the reason she'd run?

Laa, b'Ellahi. He couldn't. He *knew* the truth.

Still, whatever her motives then, for some maddening reason, against a hundred insisting he shouldn't, he believed her fear now. Worse, he had no desire to see her so anguished. Though he had every right to hurt her, he didn't want to. Not this way.

Damning himself for a fool a thousand times for feeling he should kneel and beg her forgiveness for making her feel this way he rasped, "I won't take her away. Now stop crying."

Among the crashing in her head, the detonations tearing apart her chest, Carmen heard him say, "I won't take her away."

Suddenly there was silence. And darkness.

From a timeless void, sounds returned. Blood drumming in her ears to a sluggish rhythm. Another set of heartbeats booming there. Slow, steady, powerful. Coming from the living granite wall her ear was pressed against.

The rest of her senses coalesced. Smell, soaking in the scent of virility and vigor. Touch, transmitting the luxury of cashmere and silk and power. Orientation, placing her in his embrace, her head on his chest, her breasts molded against his upper abdomen, his arms around her back, her thighs. Then her sight focused on the fierceness drawing his winged eyebrows together, chiseling his features deeper, clouding the translucence of his golden eyes.

Such *intent*. He was carrying her to yet another session of delirium and ecstasy. The tension that had started to gather in her limbs melted into the enervation of expectation, her body readying itself for his onslaught, his possession…

But as each of his strides transmitted their effortless power to her bones, realization seeped through, until everything crashed back into her awareness.

This wasn't the past. He wasn't carrying her to his bed, or anywhere else where he'd ravish her with pleasure. This was now. In the oppressive present.

She might have imagined the words he'd said pledging he wouldn't take Mennah from her.

She convulsed in his arms from the resurrected dread. His scowl deepened, and his hold firmed as he shouldered open her bedroom door. "Be still. You passed out."

"Put me down. I'm all right now."

"I'll put you down on your bed. *B'Ellahi,* quit struggling."

She shook her head, crushing his lapels in spastic fingers. "You said you w-won't…?"

He didn't answer her amputated question, deposited her on her bed with utmost care, leaning over her with arms flanking her head. His eyes swept down her length as they'd always done, as if he were struggling with the decision about which part of her to ravish first.

When he had her quaking, he swept back up to her eyes, drawled, "I won't take Mennah away from you, Carmen. I'm not the monster you insist on painting me."

"I never thought you were a monster."

"No? The man you claim to think would have forced you to abort your baby, or would take her from you to banish her somewhere, make her live her life unknown and illegitimate so he'd secure his position? If this isn't a monster, what is?"

"I'm sorry, Farooq. So sorry." She clung to his forearms as he began to withdraw, desperate to make him understand. He extricated himself as if from slime. She shuddered. "I was so afraid…it was too huge, I couldn't afford a margin of error, could only consider worst-case scenarios. I was afraid you'd think I'd lied on purpose, meaning to compromise you. I didn't know you long enough to know how you'd react to perceived betrayals or threats. And then it wasn't about you, or me. It was about her. Everything is about her. She's everything to me. *Everything.*"

Emotions she couldn't define blasted from his eyes, flaying her. It was a minute before he had mercy on her. He wrenched his gaze away, razing her single bed, her room, instead. She felt him wrestling his temper under control and began to realize the depth of his affront, his fury.

Everything he'd said was the opposite of what she'd imagined. It shriveled her to know she'd taken extreme actions that had hurt him on so many levels….

No. They had hurt him on only one level—where Mennah was concerned. He suffered anger that she'd hid the baby, offense that she'd dared fear him concerning any child, even one conceived without his will and knowledge. What *they'd* shared was not worth mentioning except to reference her exit act, which he'd made clear had been so pathetic he'd seen right through it.

Suddenly a gurgle tore through the silence. One of the sounds Carmen lived to hear. Mennah's. As if she was right between them.

Farooq stiffened, his eyes slamming back to hers for a moment of incomprehension. The sounds continued, the cooing and burbling with which Mennah entertained herself upon waking up. Astonishment invaded his eyes as they fell on the miniature receiver buckled on Carmen's waistband. Then he murmured, clearly not to her, his deepest baritone soft with amazement, "*Ya Ullah,* she's awake…"

He exploded to his feet and toward the nursery right next door. Strength flooded Carmen's limbs and she flew after him, catching his arm as his hand gripped the door handle.

"Let me go in first."

His gaze burned down on her for a moment, accentuated by Mennah's happy babblings emanating from the receiver and through the door. The feel of his muscles flexing in her grasp screamed down her nerves.

He turned away, a shake of his arm making her hands fall away like shedded leaves, making her believe he'd disregard her request.

He stared sightlessly at the door for one more moment then exhaled heavily. "*Zain.* Fine. Again I ask you to show me my daughter, Carmen. I hope you won't faint again to put it off."

Her body heat shot up another notch, this time not with awareness. "You think I was pretending?"

A growl rumbled from his gut, impatience made into sound. "Does it matter what I think?" Before she cried out a denial he ground on, "*Laaken Laa…*no, I don't think even you can pretend such a dead faint. Now quit stalling."

"Great," she grumbled. "To be exonerated from a con, only because you think my acting abilities aren't up to pulling it off. And I'm not stalling. You think I'd leave her alone for long even to thwart you? Now, can you move aside? I'll call you in when…"

He seemed to expand, blocking her way like a barricade. "I'm letting you walk in *ahead,* not *alone.* Don't test my patience anymore, Carmen."

"Or you'll do what?" she bristled.

He raised both eyebrows. "So, the falling-apart act is over and now comes…what? The hellcat one?"

She exhaled forcibly, letting out some of her tension. She couldn't walk into Mennah's nursery seething. "Who's wasting time now? Now move out of my way so I can go to my daughter. She's content to lie in her crib yammering to herself when she wakes up, but I never leave her alone for more than a few minutes."

He gave a theatrical gesture, inviting her to precede him.

She opened the door a crack.

"You make her sleep in the dark!"

The hiss lodged between her shoulder blades. She closed the door, glared up at him. "You have a problem with that?"

His scowl was spectacular. "You should leave a nightlight on. She'll get scared if she wakes up in pitch-black like that."

Her lips twisted. "And this is your expert opinion as an experienced dad?" Again the growl rumbled from in his gut, softer, no doubt because he feared Mennah might hear. She challenged him again. "Does she sound scared to you?"

His jaw muscles clenched in what she could only describe as grudging concession.

God, had he always looked that—that indescribable?

Struggling to bring yet another pang of response under control, she found herself saying, "My mother never made me sleep in the dark, and I developed a phobia of darkness. It took me years of agonizing self-conditioning to get over it."

Why was she explaining her actions as if she was defending her maternal ability? He could hear with his own ears that Mennah wasn't in the least disturbed to be awake in a dark room, had already conceded that, no matter how unwillingly.

And what was that strange expression that flared in the depths of those lion's eyes of his?

Slowly she started to reopen the door. He took the door

from her, closed it again. "This is the first time you've mentioned your mother."

She stared up at him, huffed a sarcastic breath. "And you're what? Surprised I had one?"

"Had?" he probed. "She's dead?"

She nodded, her throat closing all over again. "Cancer."

"When?"

"Just over ten years now. She died on my sixteenth birthday."

His eyes narrowed, the amber intensifying. "On the very day?"

She nodded, tears she hadn't shed then brimming.

What was he doing, interrogating her this way? What was *she* doing, pouring out information about herself? She'd never talked about her past with him. There was so much she'd never wanted to share with others, especially someone as blessed as he was.

Their time together had been consumed in conflagrations of mindless passion. When they had talked, it had been about their tastes, fantasies, beliefs. She'd assumed he'd run a background check on her, had a full report with her statistics somewhere in his security files, one he probably hadn't bothered to read. And why should he have? He surely didn't clutter his mind with the particulars of the steady parade of women who warmed his bed. And she'd already known of his background, since he was such an international figure.

She broke contact with those eyes that made her feel turned inside out for his inspection. "We'll go in now. But I'm warning you…when Mennah sees you, she may be upset, may even cry. She doesn't like strangers."

"I'm not a stranger."

He was so close he singed her cheek, the side of her neck with the heat of his vehemence, the intoxication of his breath. She shuddered, leaned on the door.

"You're still one to her…" The words petered out on her lips, in her mind, evaporated by the intensity in his gaze.

Mennah's yammering took on an excited edge. She must have sensed them even through the noise she was making. Carmen opened the door, turned up the dimmer, drenching the cheery room in soothing illumination. Mennah let out a squeal, started kicking her legs in welcoming delight as soon as she saw Carmen.

"Oh, darling, me, too." Hungry strides took her to Mennah, before she froze. Farooq had clamped her shoulder.

Suddenly Mennah's happy noises ceased, her smiles dissolving into a look of surprise. She'd seen Farooq towering behind Carmen.

Wide-eyed, she stuffed both hands in her mouth and stared at him, chewing on her chubby fingers. Carmen felt apprehension rising, thoughts streaking over how to stop what she knew would come. The wobbling chin, the down-turning lips, the whimpers and tears and the arms outstretched for her.

She wondered why she'd want to spare him that.

The answer formed alongside the question in her mind.

She'd misjudged him, deprived him of Mennah's first precious months of life. He should have been the second person who held her, whom she saw. She should have been secure in his presence from her first moment of life, should be squealing her pleasure at the sight of him now, too. If, after Mennah's delightful welcome to her, she whined and whimpered at Farooq, Carmen didn't know what she'd…

"Ya Ullah, ma ajmalhah."

Farooq's awed words jolted through her heart. *How beautiful she is.* Being fluent in Arabic had secured her the opportunity of organizing his conference, the reason she'd met him.

He went on, in a more ragged rasp, as if to himself, *"Ma arwa'ha, hadi'l mo'jezah as'sagheerah!"*

How marvelous she is, this little miracle.

And he had no idea just how miraculous Mennah was. The baby everyone had sworn Carmen would never be able to conceive. Now, after her hysterectomy, the only baby she'd ever conceive. Mennah was beyond a miracle. She was Carmen's every reason to go on living.

Overloaded with emotion, she felt him brushing past her, watched with breath gone and heart stampeding as he leaned down in leashed eagerness, reaching one powerful finger to brush Mennah's cheek, a sound of agonized enjoyment escaping him.

Transferring his gentleness to the hands still half-stuffed in Mennah's mouth, he whispered, *"Ana abooki, ya sagheerati."*

I'm your father, my little one. Delivered in a vocal caress that was delight soaked in wonder and pride and possessiveness and a dozen other emotions.

Carmen's heart splintered.

Oh God. Oh *God.* If she'd had the least doubt before, she no longer had it. He wanted Mennah. *Fiercely* wanted her.

And she'd once had a taste of how fiercely he could want…

Her eyes snapped to Mennah, dread of her reaction mounting, every muscle ready to snatch her up at the first whimper, to soothe her, ameliorate his disappointment, promise she'd soon get used to him. Not that she had any idea how Mennah would do that, when she had no idea how he intended to be in her life from now on, at best as a long-distance father…

Mennah's piercing squeal had her heart almost kicking her off her feet. She surged forward, but Mennah was…she was… She was smiling!

And not any smile, but a huge, dimpled one. Then she was eagerly rolling to a sitting position, holding up her arms, her chubby hands closing and opening, beckoning, demanding to be picked up. By Farooq!

Farooq whooped in elation, scooped her up. *"Erefteeni, ya zakeyah!"* He held her up, his large hands spanning her rib cage. "You're so clever you recognized me at once." He tickled her and she kicked her legs, screeching sharp sounds of pleasure, reaching out both hands to his face, her palms landing anywhere. He let her paw him, his chuckles escalating into guffaws.

Suddenly he took her to his chest, enfolded her, closed his eyes on a deep, long groan. Carmen's heart swelled so fast, so hard she felt it might burst. Next moment, it almost did.

Mennah mashed her face into his neck and went still. Closed her eyes, too. As if to savor her father's feel, inhale his scent, absorb his power and protection.

And Carmen's tears wouldn't be held back anymore.

She swung around, ran out, needing to get as far as possible before a storm of anguish like those that had overcome her all through her pregnancy overtook her.

She closed the door to the bathroom, slumped on it as sobs shredded through her.

To see them together, father and daughter, to know what she'd deprived them of, to know she hadn't had to run, to endure all the pain alone, that he would have been there for her, if only for the sake of the daughter she'd been carrying…

A knock at her back almost heaped her to the floor again.

"Mennah wants to see you now, Carmen."

Farooq's voice was…tender. It had to be the distortion of hearing it through the door… But no, it was tender for Mennah. *She* would never know anything soft or indulgent from him again.

She wiped both sleeves over her eyes, ran shaking fingers through her mess of tangles. Then she opened the door and stepped back into the hall. The sight that greeted her almost sent the dammed anguish flooding again.

Farooq had discarded his jacket, now stood with shirt half unbuttoned, raven mane mussed, glossy locks raining down his leonine forehead, with Mennah perched on his left hip, looking at her gleefully as if asking her to share this incredible find, this giant she'd already twisted around her little finger. He, too, was smiling hugely. She knew it wasn't at her. This was his pleasure at holding Mennah, his whimsy at his unbridled reaction to her.

"So this is what a bundle of joy is." He looked down on Mennah, giving her a playful squeeze. She squealed, buried her face into his chest, her fingers going for the hair. He winced, his lips spreading wider with her first pull. He carefully disentangled her fingers. "*Ma beyseer, ya kanzi es-'sagheer.* It doesn't work that way, my little treasure. Your father's hairs remain where they are. Let me give you something else to maul."

He dipped into his pocket, produced what Carmen assumed was a cell phone. It had probably been designed for him. He pushed a button, had it displaying a video of animals in the wild. Mennah grabbed it in eager hands, lost interest in the moving pictures in just seconds and decided to find out if it was chewable.

Carmen groaned. "Farooq, she'll ruin it."

He gave her an imperious glance. "What if she does?"

"Oh, no, you're not!"

"I'm not what?"

"You're not walking into her life and showering her with grossly overpriced stuff and letting her tear it apart. I'm not letting you turn her into a brat who thinks nothing has value."

Imperiousness gave way to scorn. "A harping mother already?"

"A responsible adult, you mean. Maybe you don't know what that is, having been born submerged in golden spoons, but I'm not letting you do that to my daughter."

"You're contesting my parenting methods? When I haven't had ten minutes to put them into practice? You think I'll indulge her into becoming a thoughtless, useless, destructive creature? Another assumption, Carmen?"

Mennah saved Carmen from withering under his barrage by performing her favorite trick. Testing gravity. The phone clattered on the hardwood floor.

Carmen swooped down to pick it up, looked at him accusingly.

He shrugged, secured Mennah on his hip as she tried to pluck out his buttons. "It's too sturdy to be damaged by anything Mennah can do. That's why I gave it to her."

She simmered. "That's not the point. Now she'll think it's okay to throw stuff that isn't her toys around."

Imperiousness rose further. "She won't. I'll see to it."

"*I'll* see to it. As long as you don't sabotage my efforts."

Their eyes locked, dueled. Carmen felt her heat rising, her breath shortening as she hauled all the height she could into her five-foot-seven frame in answer to his straightening from his relaxed pose for their confrontation, dwarfing her in size and aura.

Challenge suddenly drained from his eyes, intimidation flooding in its wake. "Who were you waiting for?"

She blinked at the abrupt change of subject. "The super. I have a short in the laundry room. He was supposed to come fix it."

One eyebrow rose. "You make filet mignon *au champignons* for him whenever he comes to install a lightbulb?"

"It's for Mennah."

His lips twisted on derision. "Of course. Because filet mignon is a staple of a nine month old's diet."

"I gave her a taste two days ago and she's refused to nurse ever since, so I thought if I gave her another taste, she might…"

The rest of her words backed up in her throat. At the word *nurse,* his gaze moved to her breasts. Breasts that immediately throbbed, their nipples conquering the thickness of her clothes, jutting their hunger. And that he could do this to her with a look, that he should see her helpless response…

His eyes dragged back to hers, pupils almost engulfing the gold in blackness. "So you were waiting for the super. Who didn't come." She jerked a nod. "Show me your problem."

"I'm sure it's just a short. I would have investigated it myself, but I was almost electrocuted once …"

"When was that?"

"I was twelve..." She groaned. "What's with the interrogation?"

"You have quite a lot of hang-ups."

"And you what?" She kept her tone sweet for Mennah. "Think someone who has a couple of phobias shouldn't be a mother?"

He smiled down at Mennah, drawled, "You said it, not me."

"You mean you do think it!"

"I *mean* you said it, not me." The words were sharp steel, the tone softest silk. Of course for Mennah, too. "I say exactly what I mean. You'd do well to remember that, Carmen."

She held her tongue as he haughtily gestured for her to lead the way. At the laundry room, he handed her Mennah. Then, without needing a ladder, he stretched up his six-foot-five frame, examined the bulb socket by the light coming from the corridor. In a few precise actions, with the screwdriver she kept handy on a tool shelf, he dismantled it, did something to the wires inside, put everything back together, screwed the bulb back in place then flicked the switch. The light burst on.

Mennah yelped. Carmen croaked, "I'm amazed."

His lips twisted. "That I know basic maintenance techniques?"

"Considering you have hordes of people waiting on your every blink, I'm wondering why you deemed to pick up the skills."

"I was taught every survival skill early on, then made myself fully self-sufficient. I can do anything anyone does for me better than them. I only abide others' services to save precious time for the more important things only I can do."

Okay. Whoa. "So you're Sheikh MacGyver, huh?"

He smiled. But not at her, at Mennah, held out his arms to her again. Mennah pitched forward, eagerly throwing herself at him.

Carmen berated herself for her stupid reaction. He'd said he wasn't taking Mennah from her, and she shouldn't feel jealous of Mennah's instantaneous and unrestrained delight in him. He was her father. He deserved the same love Carmen got from her.

His lazy drawl aborted her chaos. "About that filet mignon..."

She gulped down the silly tears. "What about it?"

"You say Mennah loved it, and it did smell delicious when I came in. It's a pity to let it go to waste."

"You want to *eat?*"

"I've been known to indulge in the practice."

"But it's already cold."

"You do have means to reheat it, don't you?"

"Reheating will overcook it, destroy its buttery softness..."

"Let me..." He dropped a kiss on Mennah's downy cheek as if compelled before going on, "Let *us* worry about that." Suddenly all ease evaporated, suspicion flaring in eyes that slammed back into hers. "Are you sure you're not waiting for someone?"

"Someone?" she jeered, seeing red. "You mean my 'sponsor'? One of many, no doubt. You think I entertain men in rotation, a few feet from my sleeping infant? Why don't you just call me a whore? C'mon, get it off your chest. I know how men of your culture view easy women and I *was* easy, with you. But I never let you 'sponsor' me. Oh wait, I did. I shared your 'privileges.' But surely you didn't think that was enough for me. You must have checked your collection of priceless cuff links to make sure I hadn't 'shared' more than your hundred-star existence. I trust you weren't too disappointed to find everything accounted for."

His eyes spat danger, sending a frisson of anxiety radiating through her limbs. "Such caustic wit and a rapier tongue. You hid them well."

"I didn't hide them. There was no reason for them to surface. You weren't a domineering brute back then."

The flames in his eyes leaped. "The domineering brute would have walked in here with bodyguards and diplomatic attachés, snatched his daughter and walked out over your weeping, begging body. *I* am still waiting for you to remember basic courtesy and invite me to share the meal you were preparing when I arrived."

And if it were possible to die of mortification, she would have keeled over.

Embarrassed, cornered and mad as hell about it, and at him, she mumbled sourly, "Okay. Fine. But if the meat is leathery and the sauce is congealed, I don't want to hear it."

He pursed his lips. "Eat in silence, you mean?"

She rolled her eyes. "As if."

He smiled then—a slow, hot smile, all for her this time, amused at her wisecrack.

She didn't know what held her up all the way to the kitchen.

Once there she shakily tried to take Mennah to put her in her high chair. He declined, did it himself as if he'd been doing it every day. Then, without being told, he placed Mennah's toys on her tray and she immediately began the game of throw and fetch.

After her bones solidified enough in her limbs, Carmen began the reheating procedure then turned around, only to be stabbed in the heart again by the poignant sight Farooq and Mennah made together, so alike, sharing such an elemental, almost tangible bond.

She located something resembling her voice. "You're taking to your father role spectacularly. And I've never seen her like this with anyone. Not that she's seen many people."

"She recognized me. As I did her. The bond is…elemental."

What she'd just thought. "Yes," she choked. "And I—I'm truly sorry for depriving you of-of…" She made a helpless gesture at them, her hand trembling. "This. But please believe I thought I was doing the best thing. For her."

He said nothing to that. Not out loud. His eyes said he believed nothing she said.

Oh, well. He wouldn't get over his anger that fast.

She inhaled before she blacked out. "I'll cooperate in any way so you'll be a part of her life, be with her whenever possible."

"I will be with her always." This wasn't a statement. This was a pledge. A decree.

"A-always? B-but you live halfway across the globe…"

His gaze hardened. "And so will she."

"But you said…"

"I said I won't take her from you, and I won't. You will both be with me. We will marry."

Four

Something was burning.

Was that her sanity going up in flames? Why else could she have imagined he'd said—said...

We will marry.

But she wasn't imagining him exploding from his relaxed pose by Mennah's high chair and...charging at her...

She blinked as he zoomed toward her, couldn't even brace herself, couldn't think, blink, breathe.

Next second he bypassed her. She whirled around in the draft of his movement, uncomprehending, watching as he yanked the pan off the stove, quickly poured its contents onto the serving plate she'd prepared before turning off the flames.

Then he looked at her, one eyebrow raised disapprovingly. "You seem bound on not feeding me this filet mignon."

Carmen stared at him. Had he really said *we will marry?*

But how? *Why?* He didn't want her. Or at least, he'd never wanted her for more than a passing diversion. He—he...

He was doing this for Mennah.

Comprehension materialized like a jagged rock inside her heart, expanding outward, tearing it apart.

She might have loved him at first glance, but she'd never entertained the fantasy of being his in any way but a fleeting one. That he should be offering the ultimate commitment, no matter the cause, and no matter that he wasn't actually offering, but decreeing it, was…was…

Her mind screeched to another halt.

Oblivious to the effect of the bomb he'd just dropped on her, Farooq bent to the serving plate then straightened, crowding her view, draining the spacious kitchen of light and oxygen. Or she might be about to pass out again…

"Your efforts weren't successful. I believe the dish is still edible. All it now needs is a hostess who deems to serve it."

She gulped, kept staring, frozen.

"Well?"

It was the way he said it. The condescension was too much. She smirked. "Didn't you brag about not needing people to serve you? Why don't you serve it yourself? Or are you handy only with macho stuff? Is serving food a lowly female chore?"

He stared at her as if she'd grown another head.

No wonder. He must be shocked that she could still talk. She knew *she* was. And more, that she could talk to him that way. No doubt people didn't dare sneeze in his presence.

Mennah squealed, demanding their attention. And again this incredible transformation came over his face. His very vibe changed to a soothing transmission as he turned to Mennah with a smile that tampered with Carmen's heart and brain function all over again.

"You heard that, *ya sagheerati?* Your mother thinks she can get away with anything as long as you're around." He turned eyes heavy with disturbing things on Carmen. "She forgets there will be times when you won't be."

The sheer danger of the sensuality infusing his words

kicked into Carmen's heart and loins. It made her melt. It made her mad. It made her reckless.

She tossed her head, straightened from her swooning position. "You really know nothing about me if you think I'd use Mennah as a shield—or as anything. And I need no shields against you."

"You don't?" His stare was all mock-serious interest, giving her more rope. "Are you certain about that?"

Oh God, what was she doing, provoking him this way? She knew she was no match for him, even in her own country. No one was a match for him, anywhere. He was just too powerful, as a diplomat, a tycoon and royalty. She was audaciously speaking her mind counting not on Mennah's presence but on his restraint, his basic benevolence. Both qualities she'd already strained to the limit.

But there was no stopping her now. After the upheaval of the last hour, her emotions were hurtling at the speed of her chaotic thoughts, without brakes.

"It's clear you have an ego of planetary proportions," she taunted. "You must have Atlas-level strength to be able to lug it around. And to think I once contributed to expanding it."

His gaze scraped down her body, making her feel he'd taken off every scrap of clothes, leaving her exposed, vulnerable. "You think your being the first and only woman to ever end a liaison with me contributed to my cosmic ego?"

Was that an edge of bitterness? Had her desertion meant something to him after all, on a personal level?

No. This intensity must be the outrage of a prince who expected people to prostrate themselves before him, who couldn't believe that, for whatever reason, she hadn't, just that once.

She shrugged, all artificial animation and contentiousness draining out of her. "Oh, I'm sure I caused a chink in it. One that could be detected with a microscope."

"We're talking galactic scope. Don't you mean a telescope?"

"Whatever." She exhaled, ran both hands through her hair. "I'm sure your ego is satisfied, now that you know why I did end it."

His eyes followed her movements, the way her shirt stretched over her breasts, spiking her arousal as he drawled, "Oh, I'm not satisfied. You'll have to work to that end. Hard. And long."

And it detonated in her every cell. The memory of every sensation, every tremor of the ecstasy he'd inundated her with, how hard and how long he'd done it, taking her the way she hadn't known she'd needed to be taken, giving her far beyond what she'd imagined she could be given or thought she could withstand.

Her legs wobbled, sending her groping for the counter's support. "If you feel that strongly when only your ego is involved, you take yourself way too seriously. You must try the occasional letdown, maybe even criticism. Very therapeutic."

In answer, he picked up the serving plate, prowled toward her like a panther measuring the moment he'd pounce, savoring the kill. He looked at Mennah. "Your mother is being very brave, Mennah. Or very foolish. Or she knows exactly what she's asking for."

"I'm only asking that you—that you—" The rest struck in her throat. He was nearing her as if he intended to collide into her.

"That I what? Take you up on your challenge?"

She leaned back. At the last moment he slowed, imprinting his body on hers as he reached around her with a hand holding the plate, the other joining it, imprisoning her with an arm on either side as he put the plate on the counter behind her. She once again felt something burning. Her skin this time. Her nerves.

He looked down into her shocked eyes, the gold of his turned to lava. "Wise of you to know when to stop."

Before she showed him just how unwise she was and answered with something inflammatory, he leaned harder into her, pressing his erection into her midriff.

Before she could process that he was aroused, berate

herself for the surge of elation that she affected him still, he pulled back, pulled up the high stool for her, his gaze steady on hers, telling her to sit down and shut up.

As if she could talk now, still feeling his potency digging into her, liquefying her insides. She sat. More like collapsed. Not to obey him or the voice of reason, but because she no longer had solid bones inside her limbs.

She watched with surreal fatalism as he served the filet. Until she noticed he'd taken two thirds himself.

"Relative body mass," he murmured at her glare. "But I'll feed Mennah from my share. Let's see what she can consume."

He sat down beside her, picked up a knife and fork and sampled a piece of the filet. His eyes rose to hers in surprise.

"It's even more delicious than it smells." Before she voiced the crack that catapulted to her tongue, he turned to Mennah. "And you, *ya kanzi,* are so clever you knew how good it is, how to ask for more." He cut a tiny piece over and over, mincing it. "Open up, here comes more…" He carefully forked it into Mennah's eager mouth.

Carmen tensed, ready to jump if Mennah choked, felt Farooq's echoing vigilance. Mennah gulped it down easily, asked for more in delighted shrieks. He chuckled, complied at once.

It didn't even occur to Carmen to eat as she watched father and daughter demolishing his portion. It wasn't until he turned enquiring eyes on her that she realized she was gaping at them.

At that moment Mennah repeated her sudden sleeping maneuver making him relieve her from his silent interrogation, his eyes captured by Mennah once again. And once again the tenderness there shocked Carmen. It was something that, despite his generous ways with her in the past, she hadn't suspected he was capable of.

"Does she always fall asleep that suddenly?"

Carmen could only nod. His lips melted with indulgence as he rose and removed Mennah from her chair, then, enfolding her, walked out of the kitchen. It took Carmen a minute to lurch after him. She caught up with him as he exited the nursery.

He closed the door, said without preamble, "You don't need to pack anything. Make a list of your needs and everything will be at the palace on our arrival in Judar. If you forget anything, order it and it will be brought to you within the hour. After you've settled in, I'll order major store managers to come to the palace with their catalogs for you to pick whatever you wish."

She stared at him. "What are you talking about?"

An edge hardened his rich, dark tone. "We're leaving right away. My jet should be ready for the return trip."

She felt the tethers of her sanity snapping one by one, groped for an anchor against his sweeping incursion. "Listen—"

He cut her off. "If you decide you feel nostalgic about your things, I'll send people to pack every shred you have here later."

"Now wait a minute. I'm going nowhere…."

"You are going exactly where I take you. To my kingdom."

She shook her head, groped for breath. "I—I can't travel…my passport isn't valid…."

"I don't need one to take you out of the country and into mine. My word is enough. Anyway, I'll arrange for one. It will be waiting for you when we arrive at my home."

"I'm not leaving *my* home."

"You are. In case you haven't grasped it yet, I'm having Mennah. Since you are her mother, this means having you, too."

His declaration felt like a slap. A stab.

A hurricane of emotions started churning inside her.

Even if he had wanted her for real, she would have been in turmoil. He wasn't just the man she loved—had *thought* she loved—he was a prince from another culture. She had no idea what being his wife entailed. But to have him state his intentions this way, as if she could have been anyone he'd endure now that he'd accidentally impregnated her, that she *was* just an unwanted accessory that came with the daughter he wanted so much…

Trying to hide her humiliation from his all-seeing eyes, she tried to scoff, "Phew, I hope this isn't how you make your peace proposals. Your region would be up in flames within the hour."

He gave her a serene look. "I save my cajoling powers for negotiations. This isn't one, Carmen. It's a decree. You had my child. You will be my wife."

The world began to tilt, overturn, nausea rising with his deepening coldness and clinical unconcern.

She somehow found her voice again, found something logical to say. "Okay, I appreciate the strength of your commitment to Mennah. But if you want to be her father, you can do that without going overboard. Parents share a child's upbringing without being married all the time, all over the world."

"I'd never be a long-distance father. My daughter will be brought up in my home, my land, exposed daily to my love and caring, taught her privileges and duties as a princess with her first steps and words. But for her best mental and psychological health, she also needs her mother constantly with her. By marrying you, that's what I'm providing for her."

Put that way, what he'd said was incontestable. But... "This can all happen without marriage. I don't want to live in Judar, but I would for Mennah. We can both always be there for her."

"And what would she be if you don't marry me? My love child? Do I even need to state that a marriage, to give her her legitimacy, her birthright, is beyond question?"

"But I..." The quicksand beneath her feet snatched at her. And she cried, "I don't want to get married ever again!"

Carmen's vehemence hit Farooq like a gut punch.

He'd been fighting the urge to close his eyes every time she spoke, to savor that voice that could bring a man to his knees begging to hear it moaning his name.

That was until she'd said...

"You've been married before?" he rasped.

Her face contorted before she looked away.

Something hideous sank its fangs into him. Jealousy? Why? When he'd long known everything they'd shared had been a sham?

He knew why. His instincts still insisted he'd been her first passionate involvement. How could they be so misled? Even after she'd claimed he'd been one in a hundred? How did they still insist *that* had been the lie, and what he'd felt when she'd abandoned herself in his arms had been the truth?

But her upheaval indicated true involvement. A husband who'd meant so much, his mere memory brought that much pain.

Another thought struck him with such violence he wanted to drive his fist through the wall. Had she been on the rebound when she'd accepted Tareq's mission? Had her seeming abandon been part of her efforts to forget the man she'd loved?

"When were you married?"

At his question, she kept her eyes averted until he thought she'd ignore him.

Then a whisper wavered from her. "I wasn't yet twenty. He was three years older. We met in college."

"Young love, eh?"

Her color rose at his sarcasm. "So I thought. Long before he divorced me three years later, I realized there was no such thing."

So *he'd* divorced *her.* And she was still hurt and humiliated that he had. But if she'd been twenty-three then, she'd met *him* two years afterward. Had she still been pining for her ex then?

But what man could have walked away from her? *He* wouldn't have been able to. Hell, he'd been willing to marry her. Granted, he would never have gone as far as marriage if it hadn't been what was best for Judar, but she'd been the only one he could have considered for such a permanent position in his life, the only one he'd wanted in his bed indefinitely.

"I swore I'd never marry again."

Emotions seethed at her tremulous declaration. "Don't you think it's extreme to swear off marriage after such a premature and short-lived one? You're still too young to make such a sweeping, final vow. You'll still be young ten years from now."

She shook her head. "It has nothing to do with age. I realized marriage isn't for me. I should have known from my parents' example that marriage is something that's bound to fail, no matter how rosily everything starts."

"Your parents' marriage fell apart, too?"

"Yeah." She leaned on the wall, let out a ragged breath. "Theirs lasted a whopping five years. Half of them in escalating misery. I was only four and I still remember their rows."

"So you have a couple of bad examples and you think the marriage institution is set up for failure?"

Her full lips twisted, making his tingle. But it was the assessing glance she gave him that made him see himself taking her against the wall. "Don't *you?* You're—what? Mid-thirties? And you're a sheikh from a culture that views marriage as *the* basis for life, urges youths to marry as early as possible and a prince who must have constant pressure to produce heirs. You must have a worse opinion of marriage than mine to have evaded it this long, to be proposing a marriage as a necessary evil to solve a problem. Uh…make that a potential catastrophe."

He gritted his teeth. "Marriage, like every other undertaking, is what you make of it. It's all about your expectations going in, your actions and reactions while undertaking it. But it's mainly hinged on the reasons you enter it."

"Oh, my reasons were classic. I thought I loved him. I thought he loved me. I was wrong."

"Then you were responsible for that failure, since you didn't know him or yourself well enough to make an informed decision. And then, love is the worst reason there is to enter a marriage."

"I can't agree more now. But I know *us* well enough to know that what you're proposing is even crazier, and your reasons are even worse. At least I married with the best of intentions."

"Those famous for leading to hell? Figures. But my reasons are the best possible reasons for me to marry at all. They don't focus on impossible ideals and fantasies of happily-ever-afters and are, therefore, solid. Our marriage won't be anything like the failure you set yourself up for when you made a wrong choice."

"And you think this isn't another one?"

Another argument surged to his lips, fizzled out.

What was he doing, trying to change her mind? This wasn't about her, neither was it about him. This was about Mennah. And Judar. What they wanted didn't feature into the equation.

"This *isn't* a choice. There isn't one," he said.

"There has to be!" she cried, her eyes that of a cornered cat. "And—and you're a prince. You can't marry a divorcee!"

"I can marry whomever I see fit. And you are my daughter's mother. This is the only reason I'm marrying you. What's more, I will declare that we are already married, have been from the beginning. Now we'll exchange vows."

"Ex-exchange vows? But—but we can't do that!"

"Yes, we can. It's called *az-zawaj al orfi,* a secret marriage that's still binding. All it requires are two consenting adults and private vows, recited then written in two papers, a copy for each of us, declaring our intention to be married. We'll date the papers on the day I first took you to my bed. Once in Judar, we'll present these papers to the *ma'zoon,* the cleric entrusted with the chore of marrying couples and we'll make ours a public marriage."

She stared at him openmouthed. At last she huffed in incredulity. "Wow, just like that and voilà, you'll make me your wife in retrospect. Must be so cool to have that loophole with which to rewrite history. Wonder how many times you've invoked that law to make your affairs legitimate."

"Never. And I couldn't have cared less if everyone knew I'd taken you out of wedlock. Everyone knows I accept offers from the women who mill around me, and that I make sure there are never repercussions. I didn't with you. Now it's fortunate I have this method of damage control to fall back on, to reconstruct your virtue and protect Mennah from speculation on the circumstances of her conception."

Her breathing quickened as he flayed her with his words until she was hyperventilating, her color so high she seemed to glow in the subdued light of her corridor.

At last she choked, "God, you're serious." Then a strangled sound escaped her as she whirled around and ran.

He stared after her, his body throbbing, his nostrils flaring on her lingering scent.

If he'd thought he'd wanted her in the past, that was nothing to what he felt now. It was as if knowing all the ecstasy they'd wrung from each other's bodies had blossomed into a little living miracle had turned his hunger into compulsion.

And then there was the way she was resisting him.

That was certainly the last response he'd expect from any woman to whom he deemed to offer marriage. And he'd only ever thought of offering it to Carmen. She'd thwarted him the first time he'd been about to offer it. Now that he had, she seemed to think throwing herself off a cliff was a preferable fate.

It baffled him. Enraged him. Intrigued him. Aroused him beyond reason. It wasn't ego to say he knew that any woman would be in ecstasy at the prospect of marrying him. As a tycoon and a prince, he assured a life of undreamed of luxuries. So what could be behind Carmen's reluctance and horror?

He entered her bedroom, found her facedown on her bed, her hair a shroud of silk garnet around her lushness, her body quaking with erratic shudders.

Was it upheaval over her ex? Was it fear of, or allegiance to Tareq? Was this another act? Or was it something else altogether?

No matter what her reasons were for being so averse, they were of no consequence. He didn't just want to pulverize her resistance, he *needed* to. It was like a red flag to an already enraged bull.

He came down beside her on the bed and she lurched, tried to scramble away from him. He caught her, turned her on her back, captured her hands, entwined their fingers then slowly stretched her arms up over her head. She struggled, arching up in her efforts to escape his grip. She only brought her luxurious breasts writhing against his chest. He barely stopped himself from tearing open his shirt, tearing her out of hers and settling his aching flesh on top of hers, rubbing against her until she begged for the ravaging of his hands and lips and teeth, until she screamed for the invasion of his manhood. That would come later.

But she was panting, whimpering, twisting in his hold, and his intentions to postpone his pleasure, her possession, dwindled with each wave of stimulation her movements elicited.

He had to stop her, before he gave in.

He moved over her, imprisoning her beneath him. She went still as if he'd knocked her out. Anxious that he might be suffocating her, he rose on both arms, removing his upper body from hers, found her eyes the color of his kingdom's twilight. She wasn't breathing.

Before he took her lips, forced his breath into her lungs, he grated, "Now repeat after me, Carmen. *Zao'wajtokah nafsi*—I give you myself in marriage."

She tossed her head on the bed, writhing again. He pressed harder between her splayed thighs, fighting not to reach down and take hold of her hips, tilt her, thrust at her as his body was roaring for him to do. Even without seeking her heat with his hardness, the pressure he exerted still wrenched dueling moans from their throats. "*Say* it, Carmen. *Zao'wajtokah nafsi*."

"God, Farooq…" she pleaded. "Be reasonable. You don't want to marry me. We can find another way…"

"There is no other way. Now say it, Carmen."

Her stricken eyes meshed with his, her flesh burning

beneath him, reminding him of all he'd once had with her, the overwhelming hunger, the affinity he hadn't been able to duplicate with anyone else. He knew that, if he wanted, he'd be buried inside her in seconds, would find her molten for him, knew she'd attain her first orgasm as soon as he thrust inside her. He could get her to promise anything when he was inside her. But he didn't want her consent that way. "Say it, Carmen. For Mennah."

At hearing Mennah's name issue from him like an invocation, she went still beneath him again.

Staring at him with eyes now the color of his kingdom's seas in a storm, she finally nodded her acquiescence, her defeat. *"Zao-zao'wajtokah nafsi…"*

Triumph roared in his system, her quavering words the most coveted conquest he'd ever made. *"Wa ana qabeltu zawajek."* He heard the elation in his voice, was unable to leash it in, saw her wincing at its harshness. "And I accept your marriage. *Alas'sadaq el mossammah bai'nanah*—on the terms we name between us. Again, Carmen, what are your demands? Make them."

"I just want Mennah."

"And you will always have her. What else do you want?"

"I don't want anything."

She was lying again. She had to be. She wanted luxuries and privileges, like any woman. That was why she'd been with him. Why she'd betrayed him. But she knew she'd get them by default being his wife, was pretending she cared nothing for them. A trick as old as woman.

She was also lying about something else. She wanted *him.* He could smell her arousal, feel the need for satisfaction tearing through her as it was tearing through him. He'd soon give it to her, give her everything she wanted. He'd have it all, too.

He'd give his daughter his love, her birthright. And he'd quench his lust for Carmen until he was sated. He'd relegate her to the role of Mennah's mother when he had no more use for her.

He might even divorce her if he wished. He didn't need her consent for that. He'd decide it, and it would be done.

But if his memories of what they'd had were anywhere near accurate, if the agony he was in at the moment was any indication, that wouldn't happen for a long time yet.

A very long time.

Five

"Will you need anything else, *ya Somow'el Ameerah?*"

Carmen squinted up at the thin, dark, bird-of-prey-like man who stood above her, body language loud with deference.

He'd called her *Somow'el Ameerah*. Again. She couldn't get her head around it. Wondered if she ever would.

It had been *Somow'el Ameer* Farooq this and *Somow'el Ameer* Farooq that since they'd set foot outside her building. All the way out of the country. It *had* taken his word—well, under a dozen words—to get her out of there. It had taken even less to make her *Somow'el Ameerah*. Highness of the princess. Her royal highness in Arabic. He'd waved his magic wand and made her a princess....

It had really happened. He'd stormed into her life, had uprooted her existence all over again.

He'd literally uprooted it this time. He'd snatched her from her home, from her country, from everything she knew, had soared with her to the unknown. And she had a feeling she'd never be back. Not for more than visits anyway. And since she had no one to visit anymore, she doubted she'd even be back at all...

Her lungs emptied as another breaker of anxiety slammed into her, pushing her under, the foreboding of stepping into the quicksand of Farooq's existence pulling at her, the forces synergizing, paralyzing her under their onslaught.

Oh God, what had she let herself in for?

She was on board his jet, on her way to Judar. There was no going back, no way out, now or ever...

"Ameerati?"

The concern in that word slowed down the spiral of agitation. The man with the hawk's face and eyes was doing it again. Probing her with solicitude, scanning her with an insight she'd bet could read her thoughts. She'd also bet he'd seen through Farooq's declaration that he'd reclaimed his wife and child, ending the misunderstanding that had led to their separation.

She remembered him well. He'd been there from the first time she'd seen Farooq, his shadow. Hashem. Farooq had told her to ask Hashem for anything in his absence. He was the only one Farooq trusted implicitly, in allegiance and ability, discretion and judgment.

Had he trusted him with the truth? Or had the shrewd man worked it out for himself? Or was everything obvious to everyone?

What did any of that matter? Hashem would take what he thought to his grave, would reinforce his prince's version of the truth with his last breath. No one else would dare even think but what Farooq had declared to be the truth.

"Ameerati—are you maybe suffering from air-sickness?"

Carmen winced at his gentleness. It made her realize how raw she was, how vulnerable she must seem to him. She shook her head.

His gaze was eloquent with his belief that she needed many things but couldn't bring herself to ask for any.

"Please, don't hesitate to ask me anything at all. *Maolai Walai'el Ahd* wants you to have all you need till he rejoins you."

Smart man. Being the über P.A. that he was, he knew the best way to make her succumb to his coddling was invoking his master's wishes, the master he'd called…

Maolai Walai'el Ahd.

Carmen started, the three words that had flowed on his tongue with such reverence erasing all she'd heard before and after them, blasting away what remained of her fugue, blaring in her mind.

Had she misheard? Was her Arabic translation center offline…?

She'd heard just fine. All her senses had been functioning to capacity since she'd set eyes on Farooq. In fact, she felt she was developing hypersensory powers. Everything was amplified, sharpened, heightening the impact of every stimulus, yanking responses from her that ranged from agitation to anguish.

Her translation center was fine, too. That was the sturdiest part in her brain. She understood what *Maolai Walai'el Ahd* meant all right. It was literally my lord successor of the Era. Aka, crown prince.

Farooq was the crown prince now?

But how? A year and a half ago, he'd been only second-in-line to the throne of Judar. What had happened to the first-in-line?

This information jogged another in her mind, igniting it with new relevance. The king of Judar was ill. From all reports there wasn't much optimism regarding his return to health. And if he died…

Farooq would soon become king of Judar.

And she'd graduate from plain Ms. Carmen McArthur to *somow'el Ameerah to Maolati'l Malekah* in no time flat.

Malekah. Queen. Yeah, sure.

The preposterousness of the whole thing burst out of her.

Hashem's dark eyes rounded at her outburst. Self-possessed as he was, she'd managed to shock him.

Yeah, him and her both. In fact, the cackles tearing out of her shocked her more than they could him.

"Ameerati?"

His bewilderment, the way he kept calling her "my princess," spiked the absurdity of it all. She spluttered under an attack of hysteria, felt her sides about to burst with its merciless pressure. "I'm s-sorry, Hashem, I'm j-just—just…"

It was no use. She was unable to stem the racking laughter, to muster breath enough to form a coherent sentence.

The man stood before her, watching her with heavy eyes that seemed to fathom her to her psyche's last spark, until she lay back in her seat, trembling with the passing of the fit as if in the aftermath of a seizure.

"God, you must think me a total flake," she wheezed.

"I think no such thing," he countered at once, his voice a soothing flow of empathy that jarred her.

God, she would have preferred anything to bristle at, to brace against. His kindness only knocked her support from beneath her, left her sinking. She hated it. She'd survived by counting on no one's goodwill, by doing without support of any kind. She had to keep it that way, now more than ever. Or she'd be destroyed.

"I apologize if my surprise gave you the impression that such an unfavorable opinion crossed my mind for a second, when the exact opposite is true. I fully realize how overwhelmed you must be. Everything has happened so fast, and *Maolai Walai'el Ahd* is formidable—and, when he has his sights on a goal, inexorable." This man *was* all-seeing. And they sure saw eye to eye in evaluating Farooq. "But he is also magnanimous and just. You have no reason to feel apprehensive, *ya Ameerati*. Everything will be fine."

Okay, here was where their concord ended. Even if she agreed the qualities mitigating Farooq's ruthlessness existed,

Hashem didn't know that Farooq no longer considered her entitled to his magnanimity, was dealing out his brand of justice by using Mennah to pressure her into giving up her freedom and choices. She was also not buying Hashem's prognosis for a second.

How could everything be fine? Ever again?

She could only pray it would one day grow tolerable.

To have Hashem's allegiance as an extension of his to Farooq, mixed in with his pity for her as a casualty of his master's inescapability, a man of such insight and importance in Farooq's life, might grow comforting. Right now she had to make him leave her to her turmoil.

She answered his original question. "Thank you, Hashem. I promise to avail myself of your services if I think of anything."

With a last probing look, he bowed and walked away, obviously loath to leave her in her state without offering service or solace.

Instead of relief, the moment he disappeared from her field of vision, chaos rushed in to fill the vacuum he'd left behind. Everything her eyes fell on contributed to her imbalance.

In both her personal and professional lives, she'd lived and worked where power brokers weaved their pacts, where billionaires flaunted their assets in an addiction to competition and for leverage in business. She'd been in the bowels of private citadels, of diplomatic and hospitality fortresses. She'd studied beauty and luxury, learned their secrets and power and how to utilize their nuances to enthrall the most jaded senses, smoothing her clients' path to winning their objectives through the goodwill engendered by perfectly designed and realized events.

This jet surpassed anything she'd ever experienced in taste and sheer, mind-numbing opulence. She'd had an idea it would be something unprecedented when she'd laid eyes on it. It was surely the first bronze-finished Boeing 737 she'd ever seen. Then she'd set foot on its plush carpeting and had plunged deeper into the surrealism of being with Farooq, being introduced as his wife and deluged in the veneration of a culture that revered its royals. All her knowledge of the best that money could buy had only sent her mind boggling in appreciation of every detail around her.

She gaped again at every article of genuine art, every flawless reproduction in design, everything spanning centuries and cultures, the classical meshing with the modern, the Western with the Middle Eastern, disparate forms of beauty melding with luxury and futuristic technology in a symphony of unlikely harmony.

She fingered her seat's armrest. A panel slid open, exposing a set of buttons. Hashem had said they gave her control over all amenities, from service to entertainment to climate control. She pushed one with a screen icon. Her head snapped to the left as an eighteenth-century mural disappeared with a smooth whir to reveal a screen of a size she hadn't known had been manufactured yet.

No need to experiment further. There'd only be more wonders, a refresher course as well as a first-time close-up of Farooq's affluence and power. And this was only his transportation...

She was staring down at her sweaty palms, fighting another wave of dizziness when her senses overloaded. She almost moaned at the force of the breach. Farooq.

She didn't want to raise her eyes. Didn't want to watch him approaching, obliterating her autonomy, shrinking the world into the parameters of his presence, his desires, his decrees.

She did, saw his eyes firing with satisfaction at her slumped pose. He closed in on her like a force of nature, two men from his extensive entourage trying to keep up with him, documenting his muttered orders. They'd disappeared by the time he reached her, a partition sliding behind them to isolate the dining area where he'd seated her before going to "arrange matters" from the rest of the jet.

He looked down at her with the same intensity as he had when he'd been on top of her, demanding she repeat his land's ancient marriage rite.

Her heart lurched like a captured bird in her chest.

Oh God, she'd really done it.

She'd really married him.

She'd lain beneath him, feeling him imprinting her, hard with an indiscriminate reaction to feeling a female body beneath him, had repeated the words that had bound her to him in a marriage without love or respect—or anything, really. A sham. A cold-blooded ruling on his part, a capitulation on hers.

It's all for Mennah. It's all for Mennah.

Maybe if she repeated the mantra enough she could endure this. The feeling of forever plummeting into an abyss.

She snatched her gaze away from his, fingered Mennah's baby monitor receiver, praying for her daughter to wake up so she could run to her and be spared another exposure to Farooq.

All she heard over the amazingly low drone of the jet's engines was the soothing Middle Eastern music through the surround sound system, and Mennah's soft breathing.

Mennah had awakened during their departure, had bubbled with excitement in response to Farooq's delight in her all through the trip in his limousine right up to the jet and through takeoff. She'd executed her sudden sleeping maneuver an hour ago, and he'd secured her car seat in one of the jet's bedroom suites.

"You haven't eaten."

At his rebuke, her eyes fell on the masculine, square-cut silver service set and cutlery, laid out before her on midnight-blue silk tablecloth, nestling among sparkling crystal and crisp white napkins. She'd picked something from the extensive menu Hashem had provided. It had been served with great fanfare under polished brass domes, placed to simmer over gentle flames. Hashem had raised the covers to show her the cookbook perfection below and the aromas of the haute cuisine creations had hit her salivary glands. Her stomach had fed on its emptiness, churned with revulsion against being catered to as if she was a beloved mistress when she was just a necessary evil, an abhorred hostage.

Corrosion surged again in her throat. "I'm not hungry."

His jaw hardened. "You haven't eaten in the last seven hours. Your stomach must be feeding on itself by now."

Gee. What was it with men suddenly being able to read her mind? Or was she just too predictable to live?

"You'll have to excuse my stomach if it isn't functioning to your calculated expectations. After all that's happened in said seven hours, all it feels now is the urge to heave out its nonexistent contents. Just imagine what it would do to existent ones."

"You're trying to tell me I make you nauseous?" Exasperation flashed across his face before morphing into derision. "Still playing games? Still challenging me to expose your proclamations for the feminine taunts that they are?"

She pressed a fist to her head in an attempt to mitigate the pressure building inside. "Just why do you want me to eat? I wouldn't miss a few pounds. If I ever manage to part with them."

His eyes changed hue, melted down her enervated body like his fingers once had, following a path of seduction, of destruction over her. "You *have* gained some weight."

She snorted. "Yeah, tell me about it."

"I will. In detail. When I'm in...possession of the full range of...particulars."

"Gee, thanks. Just what every woman wants to hear. An inventory of her expanding assets."

He leaned, ran a light touch down her left forearm to her ring finger, circled a nonexistent ring before sawing his finger between hers. "Expanding is an inaccurate word. Your assets have...appreciated." He pushed a button on her seat's armrest, swiveling it around, picked up her hand, tugged her out of her slouch, bringing her face level with his groin. "See for yourself how appreciated they are by inspecting *my* expanding assets."

A second before he had her performing a hands-on assessment, she snatched her hand from his as if he'd been forcing it into an open fire, darting a look around.

He encroached closer, coming between her legs, making her feel dwarfed, dominated. "Don't worry about accidental audience. We won't be disturbed for anything less than an impending crash. Do get on with your reconnaissance, put your mind to rest about the efficacy of your weapons."

She rolled her eyes, tried to resume breathing. "One more transparent double entendre and you win a food processor."

His lips spread on a grudging smile as his legs did the same to her knees. He leaned down, his arms braced on both sides of her head, one hand weaving into her hair, pinning her head to the seat, tilting her face upward as his descended. "Don't start a game you don't intend to play to the end."

She lurched as his breath lashed her lips, fresh and male and all him, the movement wrenching at her anchored hair, bringing tears stinging her eyes. His pupils flared, almost obliterating the irises, her name rumbling low in his chest. "Carmen..."

He was going to kiss her.

Every sensation of every time his heat and hunger had devoured her, deluged her with pleasure, drained her of will blossomed, a surround-memory replaying the glide of his flesh on hers, the taste of his tongue, of his vigor inciting her greed for more. Her heart stampeded, her lips, her nipples stung, every nerve discharged...

She couldn't sit there and pant for him to kiss her.

Her fingers landed on her armrest. The seat swiveled away, taking her out of his reach.

She felt him brooding down on her bent head for a breath-depleting moments, before he exhaled, moved away.

He lowered himself in the seat beside her, swiveling it to face hers. "More games, I see."

She huffed. "I didn't comment before because your accusation left me speechless. What games, for God's sake? The only act I ever pulled in my life was when I was out of my mind needing to get away before you found out I was pregnant. It was so transparent you must have laughed your head off every time you remembered it. I wouldn't know how to play games if I wanted to. If I did, don't you think I'd be in a better situation now?"

His eyebrows shot up. "What better situation is there? Every woman alive would kill to be in your place."

This time the laugh that tore from her hurt. "Every woman alive would kill to have her motives, her *anguish* ridiculed, her character reviled, her life railroaded?"

His gaze hardened, flared before something like amusement flooded its depths, softening the edges, putting out the fire. "Any more R words? Recounting how I routed you out, ran roughshod over you then through a bit of rough-and-tumble got you to reiterate the vows that have roped you to me, *ya rohi?*"

The endearment, *my soul,* speared her with its sarcasm. Its impossibility. The rest of his wickedness had a counteractive effect, tickling her. And she couldn't help it.

She made a face at him, stuck out her tongue. "Show off."

He threw his head back on a surprised guffaw, his face blazing with enjoyment, turning his beauty from breathtaking to heartbreaking. She found herself smiling back at him in yet another demonstration of unabashed idiocy.

And it was as if they were back to those magical times a year and a half ago, when everything between them had been rich in rapport—to use two more *R* words—when they just had to say anything and the other would understand, appreciate, the desire to please as strong as the desire to pleasure or be pleasured, the smiles flowing uncensored, unfettered.

But like any illusion, the moment of communion passed. The warmth kindling his face evaporated, the mirth drained to be replaced by the coldness that had turned him into the stranger she'd left a lifetime ago.

He finally drawled, "So you claim you're not playing games. What's this about being nauseous then? Are you going to go on a hunger strike in protest of my alleged crimes against you?"

"I *am* nauseous. If you were flying into the unknown to a strange land where you knew no one, wouldn't you be?"

His chin rose. "You know me. That's all you'll need."

She shook her head at the irony. "*Do* I know you, Farooq? In the biblical sense, you mean? Oops, wrong faith here."

He leveled his gaze on her, his eyes glinting with danger and a resurgence of reluctant humor. "You'd be surprised how alike all faiths are. And besides knowing me, thoroughly, in that sense, you know every other thing that counts."

"Really? So being the crown prince of Judar now is one of the things that don't count? I just discovered that—by accident."

His eyes narrowed. "And the discovery disappoints you?"

She sagged further in her seat. "It *staggers* me. Staggers me *more*, to be accurate. You're not just a prince, you're *the* prince. And to think I was going to pieces contemplating what being the wife of a Middle Eastern prince entailed. Now I'm scared witless at what is expected of the crown prince's wife. If I'm woefully unsuited for the first position, I'm disastrous for the second."

He looked away, presenting her with the magnificence of his slashed profile. He was silent for a long moment, looking lost in thought.

Then without looking back at her, he drawled in a distant, distracted tone, "You speak Arabic. It was why you were chosen. I never thought to ask if you did. You never spoke it, but when I thought of it later, I realized you understood when my men did, when I reverted to using it in extremes of passion."

She blinked. What was this jump in logic? And she was "chosen"? For what? But what had her heart shriveling was his indifference as he mentioned his reversion to Arabic during their intimacies. That had always sent her spiraling into mindlessness, knowing it was what had heralded his loss of control, his plunge with her into the depths of ecstasy.

When he didn't add anything more, continued staring at nothing, she had to say something. "I do speak Arabic. If you mean that's why I was chosen to organize your conference, it *was* what made me stand out, made me land such a huge opportunity. Though I'm better in the formal dialect than your colloquial Judarian—"

He cut across her aimless rambling. "You read and write it?"

Her heart dropped a beat at the sub-zero inflection in his voice. "Y-yes. Better than I speak it, actually. Pronunciation has always been a bit tricky. I'm okay I guess, but I could be better—"

He again cut her off. "Besides Arabic, you speak, read and write French, Italian, Spanish, German and Chinese?"

He'd finally read the file his security/intelligence machine must have compiled on her, had he?

She exhaled. "Yes, if not all with the same proficiency…"

"And apart from being an events planner, of which conferences of international scale were but one type of event you handle, you've worked as an interpreter, a hostess and a facilitator in the range of diplomatic functions and every other sort of multinational event. You've set up a cyberconsultancy service organizing such events, networking providers, coordinating themes, putting every detail together from the ground up from the comfort of your home."

Still unable to understand where this was leading she answered, "Yes, but how is that—"

He again aborted her query, still staring into space. "The wife of the crown prince of Judar has to be beside him in formal and informal meetings with dignitaries from around the globe. She must be acutely aware of the cultural protocols of every nation and faith, be versed in the art of etiquette and dialogue with everyone from servants to magnates, from emissaries to heads of states. She has to have an appreciation for all forms of art, an understanding of global historical landmarks, be up-to-date about contemporary world state and technologies. Mastery of seven languages which include Arabic would turn such a wife into an unprecedented find."

He looked at her then, held her stunned gaze, his giving nothing of his thoughts away. Then he drawled, "If I'd tailored a woman for the position of my wife, I wouldn't have come up with one more suited for it than you."

Six

Something frantic flapped inside Carmen's chest.

It felt too much like hope.

She pressed her palm over it, trying to stem its painful surge. Not that she knew from experience, but she'd heard that where it blossomed, hope defied logic, sprouted with a life of its own, blasted through barriers of caution and self-preservation.

It seemed to be doing so now. It kept saying, if he believed her experience and skills would be of use to him, maybe her life in Judar wouldn't be a prison of duty outside her role as Mennah's mother, and she'd find purpose and function there, in his life. And maybe—just maybe—one day they'd forge some sort of relationship, and their marriage wouldn't remain the lie he intended to propagate for Mennah's legitimacy and birthright...

"Now you heard what you're fishing for, what more reasons will you give for being 'staggered' that I'm now the crown prince?"

His disparagement hit her with the force of a landslide, smothering the chain reaction of optimism.

So he didn't believe she could be valuable to him in his new position? He'd been leading her on only to slap her down?

Shoved back into the pit of resignation, her hand shook as she raised it from her chest to her eyes, pressing the stinging away. "I already told you why I think this a huge mistake. But you've made up your mind about me and whatever I say, no matter if it's the truth, won't change it for you." She shot him what she hoped was a look of unconcern. "Why bother wasting more breath?"

His cynical pout was proof of her deductions. He still prodded, "Waste some more, just for me. Tell me your version of the 'truth.'"

"What do you care about my 'version' when you already know everything about me since the day I was born, Farooq? You're probably in possession of details I don't even remember or know."

"And how am I supposed to possess that omniscient knowledge of your life?"

"C'mon, Farooq. Your intelligence machine must provide you with a phonebook-thick dossier on everyone who comes within a hundred feet of you."

"That's true. But I don't have one on you."

He didn't? But he must have…*oh*. Oh. A sarcastic huff escaped her. "That's right. My life would fill two pages. Double spaced."

He clicked his tongue. "That's not a version of the truth, that's an outright lie, Carmen. The things I found out about you from talking to you, from *taking* you, would fill a book. I was wrong about the content of the book, but whatever the truth is, it'd still fill a book. But neither book would contain the most basic data about you, what you never divulged. And for some reason, it didn't matter and I didn't have you investigated." She knew the reason, all right. Because *she* hadn't mattered. "Then I did, but you'd erased your existence so well, I came up with only your professional portfolio, address—and a photo." His palm pressed over his heart, like hers had done minutes ago. Was that where the photo was? "Of you and Mennah."

Her eyes remained prisoner to the telling gesture, her own heart battering itself against her ribs, even when she wasn't sure what it told her.

It was his claim that he knew nothing about her that slowed her heartbeats. Could it be?

She *had* used methods learned in the circles where people erased their pasts or reinvented themselves for safety and second chances, first to cover up parts of her past to escape the heartache, then to remain hidden with Mennah forever. But she hadn't thought her cover-up tactics would be so effective that he wouldn't find out everything about her if he put his mind to it.

But then he probably hadn't; had only tried to find her, not find out *about* her. Trailing someone wasn't the same as researching them. Yes. That had to be it.

She sighed. "Well, what you came up with was enough. You found me, found out what I ran to hide. Anyway, I never tried to hide who I am from you, so you do know everything that counts."

"Really?" He mimicked her recent irony. "Beyond knowing what you can do, in your job, in bed…" The way he said that, in such menace-coated sensuality, made her snicker. He raised one eyebrow. "So glad you find me funny. Even when I'm not trying to be."

Her earlier outburst rippled to the surface, her facial muscles hurting under its renewed onslaught. "It *is* hilarious, hearing you refer to me as some sort of femme fatale."

"They don't come any more fatal, Carmen."

She looked around, looked back at him, pointed to herself

in open mockery. "You're talking about me? Boy, now *that's* a parallel universe version of the truth. A Bizzaro world one. Whom have you been talking to? Someone I turned down and he decided to paint me as a black widow? To justify his failure as he propagates tales of his lucky escape? One thing's for sure. You didn't get this from my ex. Apart from him, you're the only man who was in a position to comment on my so-called sexual powers, and you both certainly…"

Her voice trailed off. What was it with those attacks of truthfulness? Had she misplaced her discretion during the months she'd barely talked to another adult?

It was futile to kick herself over it now, anyway. She'd already said too much. The whole truth and nothing but.

Now his eyes were glinting with things that sent goose bumps cascading through her like a storm through a wheat field.

Before she could theorize what those things were, impassiveness blanked his gaze, neutralized his voice. "You're telling me I'm one of only two men in your life?"

His ego relished that, did it? So what? She was only expanding it from planetary to stellar proportions. Nothing mere mortals could tell the difference between.

"I *am* telling you that," she ground out. "And you know what, you're not only the second, you're the last."

He sat forward, coming closer like a tide that would overwhelm her if she didn't back away. "Of course I'm the last."

She didn't. "You are, because even if I wasn't off men after you and my ex, I'd never expose Mennah to a strange man."

He stilled, intensifying the menace in the calmness of his next words. "You're likening me to your ex-husband?"

She didn't care. "And it's blasphemy to liken your highness to anyone? Well, considering he's a mommy's—and daddy's—boy with loads of unearned wealth and power, the similarities are plenty. If this arouses your royal fury, it sure isn't worse than practically calling me a liar, a fraud and an all-round whore."

* * *

Farooq was lost for words for the first time. Ever.

Not because he found none to answer her insults with. What struck him mute was Carmen's allegation that he was the only man, besides the husband she'd married too early, she'd been intimate with. In effect, her only lover. The claim had flowed from her with the impetus of a statement of fact, had lodged into him with the force of an ax in the gut. Of the truth.

Could he believe it? She'd been Tareq's mole, but not his plaything? She hadn't been anybody else's? Her abandon in his arms had been just for him, as his had been just for her? Discounting the ex-husband she spoke of now without continuing emotional attachment, with disdain even, he'd been, no matter the reason, her first, and as she vowed, her last passionate involvement?

Everything in him insisted that was the truth. That she'd told him many truths today.

But she'd done so only up to a point. He could feel her hiding things. Major things. Her deal with Tareq, no doubt. And fool that he was, he didn't want to corner her into a confession.

He didn't want to hear it. Not anymore.

With each moment near her, he believed more and more that it hadn't been as sinister as he'd believed on her side, that she hadn't realized the scope of the damage she'd been sent to do. That maybe Tareq had even convinced her she'd be serving a greater good by toppling him from the succession.

If this was true, maybe Tareq had caught her at her lowest ebb, and she'd made an out-of-character decision. But once she'd succumbed to their affinity, to the pleasure they'd shared, seen him for what he was and Tareq's lies for what they were, she'd forgotten her mission. But she'd gotten pregnant and Tareq had changed the rules, and she'd panicked, feared retribution from all sides, feared for Mennah for real, had fled, hidden…

Or maybe he was looking for ways out for her because he was falling under her spell again.

And he was. Instead of the cold loathing he'd believed would be his only reaction to her, he was mesmerized by everything about her, reveling in her company, unable to get enough of her wit, her outspokenness and contentiousness and defiance, all so in contrast with the vulnerability she strove to hide. Then came her physical effect. She'd had him hard and aching within minutes of seeing her again. It was all he could do now not to drag her to the floor and just have her. Just *take* her again. And again.

He would have her. Would take her. Just not now.

He'd wait. For their wedding night.

As for the truth, whatever it was, there was nothing to be gained by ripping open festering wounds. It wasn't as if he needed to have this resolved. It was all pointless now that he'd won. Now that the throne of Judar was safe from falling into Tareq's hands. Now that she'd fallen into his. For as long as he deemed to hold her there.

And *now* he could turn to her taunt.

She dared imply he and her ex had unearned wealth and power in common? Was that how she viewed him? When she must know of the global enterprises he'd built from the ground up, multiplying his kingdom's wealth? After she'd seen for herself a six-week sample of his life as peacemaker and relief-bringer?

No. She'd meant it as the worst insult she could think of.

But even if she'd qualified it as retaliation, he'd make her pay for it. Make her beg. For the chance to atone. For the end of torment. For the pleasure he knew, just *knew*, beyond doubt, only he had ever brought her, could ever bring her.

His equilibrium regained, his mind ordered and made up once more, he challenged her, "So you take exception to my…assumptions. What others could I have when I know nothing about you beyond what your actions led me to believe?"

She seemed to shrink in her seat. "There isn't much to know. I was born to Ella and Aaron McArthur, a megawealthy businessman and his ex-P.A. second wife. Their marriage fell apart and I lived with my mother and her assortment of... strange men, until she died, then moved in with my father and his fourth wife till the day I turned eighteen. On acquiring my first boyfriend, whom I eventually married, a year later, my father, who hadn't checked to see if I was still alive since I moved out, popped back in my life all eagerness and blessings. Turned out the marriage was part of a coveted merger. When it turned out I wasn't the asset they all thought I would be, both the marriage and the merger were dissolved and my father moved to Japan with his fifth wife. When I was twenty-five, my mother's estate became mine—her accumulated alimony and divorce settlement from my father, plus what she got from her 'sponsors.' It was a bundle, the fortune you intimated I got from a 'sponsor' of my own. I bought the apartment, put the rest for Mennah in a trust fund, since I earn enough to support us both in comfort. See, I overestimated the complexity of my life. That's *one* page, triple-spaced."

Farooq stared at her, thoughts rearranging, long-entrenched ones being forced out, new questions rushing at him.

She'd been born then had been married into money. But she'd implied her father hadn't supported her after she'd moved out, that her ex-husband had divorced her without compensation. Was that why she'd accepted Tareq's mission? Had she gotten so used to the good life her mother and her "sponsors" followed by her father and her ex's wealthy family had provided that she couldn't bear to wait months till she claimed her inheritance?

That no longer felt like enough of a motive. Or a motive at all. Not with her disinterest in anything material while she'd been with him replaying in his mind, another manifestation that had the conviction, the texture of truth.

So it hadn't been about money after all? Had it been maybe

a reckless lashing out after all the major relationships in her life had failed or ended, throwing herself into something dangerous, maybe even self-destructive? She *could* have easily been throwing herself into an abyss when she'd thrown herself in his arms. She'd had no way of knowing he'd turn out to be a civilized or even sane human being, let alone the lavish lover he'd been with her. He could have been a monster who lived to collect slaves, or to abuse beauties and maim them before snuffing out their lives.

Suddenly he was incensed. Far more so than he'd ever been. At her for endangering herself that way. Whether her goal had been financial gain or temporary rebellion or oblivion.

His rage deflated as fast as it had mushroomed.

No. She might have been groping for the catharsis of a wild fling with a sheikh prince, or the fantasy of playing Mata Hari or securing a quick fortune or all combined. But she hadn't risked herself. She *had* known she'd be safe with him, would be cared for and catered to, pleasured and pampered. She'd known it, felt his nature and intentions with the first look into his eyes.

As he'd thought he'd felt her nature and intentions with the first look into hers?

But if what he'd seen was all she owned, and he could now find out the truth about her inheritance, if she still had to work, where had the money Tareq had said she'd cheated him for gone? Or had Tareq cheated *her* out of their agreed upon price?

Ya Ullah, was this how men went insane, revolving in unending loops of suspicion?

Kaffa. Enough. It didn't matter anymore, how it had been.

Suheeh? Really? If he told himself that enough times, would it register so he could finally let it go?

Another question blasted through, proving that letting go didn't seem possible. But then, it was a paramount question.

How had his people not found out all she'd just told him?

Before the question fully formed, the answer detonated in his mind. Tareq. His counterintelligence must have foiled Farooq's investigations, in fear he'd find her, find Mennah, the final card pulverizing Tareq's conspiracies to hang on to the succession.

B'Ellahi, how had he not seen this before?

Loathing for his cousin shot to a new zenith.

But anger and hatred aside, now that he knew what he had to counteract—what he might not need to counteract now that Tareq had no more reason to block his research into her past— it would be easy to check out her story. As she must know he would.

This meant one thing. She'd told him the truth.

His gaze clung to her averted profile. He no longer saw the seductress who'd breached his barriers, entrenched herself in his responses, his fantasies, his cravings, or the traitor who'd deprived him of his child, who'd almost let Judar's throne fall into the hands of a man guaranteed to topple it. He saw only the little girl who'd been exposed to her parents' damaging behavior, who grew up let down, neglected, used, maybe even abused, by everyone who should have cherished and protected her. He saw only a woman who'd suffered. A lot.

He gritted his teeth against a resurgence of fury, against all the people who'd blighted her life. Against the softening that assailed him toward her as he realized she'd been doing everything to protect her—*their* daughter, from all she'd suffered, living for Mennah, thinking only of her safety and happiness.

He might be starting to understand her motives, her psyche, but it made no difference. He couldn't forget, nor would he ever forgive what she'd done.

He exhaled, casting away the weakening, pushed a button.

It was time to get back on track.

"Are we crashing?"

Farooq turned inquiring eyes on Carmen at her croak.

She gestured toward Hashem, who'd entered their compartment carrying what looked like a treasure chest right out of the times of genies and flying carpets. "You said that's the only time we'd be disturbed."

"This is a planned intrusion." He beckoned to Hashem who strode forward, his eyes scanning her, ascertaining her condition before casting a look of disapproval on the untouched food.

Farooq rose, extended a hand to her. She must have taken it, risen, walked. Either that or he had hypnotic and/or teleportation powers, too. Without knowing how, she found herself sitting on a plush couch in yet another compartment drenched in sourceless lights and deep earth tones, in the serenity of sumptuousness and seclusion.

Hashem placed everything on a two foot-high, six-foot-wide, square polished mahogany table in front of her and Farooq. He opened the chest, produced two boxes, one the size of a shoebox, the other half its size, both like the larger chest, handmade, ornamented in complex mosaic patterns of gold, silver and mother-of-pearl. Next he produced a variegated brown leather folder and small drawstring pouch. Everything was in perfect condition, but looked ancient, heavy with history and significance.

An urge rose, to run her hands over the textures and shapes, feel their mystique and power flowing through her fingertips. She settled for soaking in each detail. The folder and pouch embossed with intricate gold-leaf borders, Judar's royal crest at their center: an eagle depicted in painstaking detail, its wings arched up to enclose the kingdom's name written in the ornamental *muthanna* or "doubled" calligraphy with each half of the design a mirror image of the other in a tear-drop oval. The boxes' blend of repoussé, inlaid and engraved *zakhrafa* embellishments that married Arabian to Ottoman, Persian and Indian designs.

Hashem's deep murmur tore her gaze back to him. She couldn't believe how welcome his presence was. How she didn't want him to leave. She couldn't take more of Farooq undiluted.

Not that an army would make effective reinforcements. Not against Farooq. Or what she felt.

Sighing, she eyed Hashem in resignation as he bowed to them and retraced his steps out of the compartment.

Farooq opened the pouch, producing two brass keys that looked designed and forged in the Saladin era. He opened the small box, produced three stamps and an inkpad of the same design, before opening the folder and extracting two papyrus-like papers and two crimson satin ribbons. Then he reached into his suit pocket—opposite the one she assumed held the photo—and extracted a gold pen.

He extended it to her. "Let's see how well you write Arabic."

She gaped from the pen to the papers to his eyes. "You're giving me a written Arabic proficiency test?"

"I am interested to see your level, yes. But I'd hardly give you royal papers reserved for documenting state matters of the highest order to test your spelling and handwriting."

So all this stuff was as momentous as she'd sensed. Her heart wrenched to a higher gear. "So what do you want me to write?"

He pushed the pen into her flaccid hand. "I'll dictate to you."

"Yeah, you live to do that, dictate," she grumbled.

One side of his lips twitched. His eyes remained solemn. "Write, Carmen."

The depth of the command, the gravity, squeezed her dry of breath. She sat forward, tremors buzzing through her like a current, took in the papers in front of her, handmade, each one a unique blend of beige-tan with multicolored fibers offsetting its pearly, heavy silk finish.

She put down the pen, wiped her hand on her pants. His clamped onto it. She bit her lip on the jolt as his other hand delved inside his jacket again, produced a monogrammed handkerchief, placed it on the paper, put the pen back in her hand.

As soon as the tremors allowed her to firm her grip on it, he started dictating. She geared her brain to the right-to-left writing of the exotic letters that always felt more like drawing.

She'd written a whole sentence before it registered.

This was a verse from a sacred scripture invocation.

She raised her hand off the paper, her eyes to his. "What is this? An incantation to sign over my soul?"

His eyes smiled now, a smile drenched in that overriding sensuality that was as integral to him as his DNA. And in seriousness. "Essentially, yes. This is *az-zawaj al orfi* language. You are free to add to the basic pledges, if you're feeling creative, to express how eager you are—were—for our union."

"This is the paper the cleric will read?"

"Yes. And along with my copy, it will reside in the royal files, proof of Mennah's legitimacy."

"So it's an official document. And you want me to get creative." The teeth sprouting in her stomach sank into its walls. "Just give me the exact language. Better yet, paraphrase."

He pouted in mockery, continued dictating. She kept writing until he told her to sign her name. She did, raised her eyes. She'd only written two paragraphs. "That's it?"

He shrugged one massive shoulder. "It takes only so many words to pledge oneself unto eternity." He reached for the paper, ran his eyes over her efforts. "I'm impressed."

Without waiting for her reaction to his praise—an upsurge of irritation for wanting it, for being so pleased at having it—he turned to his own paper, started writing the words he'd dictated her. And she forgot everything as she watched those fingers that had once owned her flesh, moving in the certainty of expertise and grace, producing a *req'uh* script of such beauty and elegance, such effect, it did feel like a spell.

After he signed both documents, had her sign his, she rasped, "So not only a prince, a tycoon, a philanthropist, a diplomat and a handyman but a calligrapher, too."

"Yet another side-product of my unearned privileged existence." His eyes mocked her, documented her chagrin at being caught out at a pettiness, at the need to apologize for it, at her anger at that need and at him.

Not that he waited for her to come to a decision about which urge to obey. He let go of her eyes, pressed three stamps to the inkpad, marked the documents with each. Judar's royal insignia, the Aal Masood family crest and the date. The one he'd fixed to the day they'd first made lo—had sex.

She stared at the seals. The dark red ink became viscous as it dried, like congealing blood. She did feel she'd just signed a blood pact. A binding, unbreakable one.

He rolled up both documents, tied each with a ribbon, placed them in the larger box. "Those papers aren't considered legitimate without two witnesses. As soon as we land in Judar, Shehab and Kamal, my brothers, will add their seals and signatures to ours." He rose, extended a hand to her. "Now we'll check on Mennah."

Everything in Carmen squeezed. Fists, guts, lungs, heart.

Mennah. The reason he'd just taken her on.

The reason she'd just signed her life away.

Seven

A gentle nudge jogged Carmen out of the twilight between exhausted sleep and strung wakefulness.

It took her a second to realize they were touching down.

Her sandpaper-lined eyes scraped open. And there he was.

Farooq sprawled opposite her, an indulgent lion letting his overzealous cub crawl all over him. He was still watching her.

He scooped Mennah up with kisses and gentleness, rose, came to stand over her. They both looked down on her from what felt like ten feet, his face opaque, Mennah's ablaze with glee.

"Do you need a few minutes to wake up, or shall we go?"

She shook her head, sprang to her feet. Her sight darkened, disappeared. His arm came around her, would have released her the moment she steadied if not for Mennah. Their daughter threw an arm over Carmen's neck, bringing the three of them into an embrace.

Carmen went limp with the blow of longing at feeling him imprinting her in such tenderness, even if borrowed, at

Mennah mashing herself against them as if seeking their protection, their union. At the hopelessness of it all.

She lurched away before her eyes leaked, held out her arms for Mennah. Mennah reached back.

Farooq only walked on. "I'll carry her."

She scampered, kept up with him. "But she wants me now."

"Do you want your mother, *ya gummuri?*" he cooed to Mennah, who looked back on Carmen with dimples at full-blast, as if she thought her father was playing catch-me-if-you-can. Carmen gave him a glare from an angle Mennah wouldn't witness. His Mennah-smile remained on his lips but his eyes frosted over. "She will see her land for the first time, be seen in it in my arms, a princess held up by her father the crown prince for all to see."

Carmen's legs gnarled with the power of image he projected, the poignancy. She rasped, "Put that way, you go right ahead."

Not that he was awaiting her approval. His strides ate up a path to the exit, leaving it up to her to keep up or not.

She scrambled in his wake, looked at the multitime zone clock on the way out: 9 a.m. in New York, 5 p.m. here. It had been sixteen hours since she'd found Farooq standing on her doorstep.

Sixteen hours. They felt like sixteen days. Sixty. Far more. It felt as if her life before those hours had been someone else's, her memories sloughing off to be replaced by another reality that had unfolded with his reappearance.

Then she stepped outside and into another world.

And it was. Though her life had taken her all over the world, Judar felt…unprecedented, hyperreal. The azure of its spring skies was clearer, more vibrant, the reds and vermilions starting to infuse the horizon as the sun descended were richer in range and depth, its breeze, even in the airport where jet exhaust should have masked everything, felt crisper, more fragrant, its very ambiance permeated by the echoes of history, the lure of roots that tugged at her through her connection with Mennah, whose blood ran thick with this kingdom's legacy.

Mennah, who seemed to recognize the place, too.

Secure in her father's power and love, she looked around, eyes wide, face rapt as she inhaled deep, as if to breathe in the new place, fathom it, make it a part of her.

Carmen knew how she felt. With her first lungful of Judarian air, she felt she'd breathed in fate.

Then she heard his voice, the voice that had steered *her* fate since she'd first heard it, that seemed would steer it forever, permeated with intensity and elation.

"Ahlann beeki fi darek, ya sagheerati."

He was welcoming Mennah home. And only her.

Carmen groped for the railing of the stairway, feeling as if a wrecking ball had swung into her.

How stupid could she get? She wanted him to welcome her home, too? When it wasn't her home, only Mennah's? When the only reason he'd brought *her* here, where he didn't want her, was Mennah? How could he welcome her where she wasn't welcome?

She nearly gagged on the toxicity of her feelings of alienation. She *had* breathed in fate, could feel it all around her. Mennah's. She was just its vehicle. Her fate was not even a consideration here.

Farooq's arm came around her shoulder.

She couldn't bear him to act the supportive husband, lurched away, continued her descent, blurted out, "I thought you were taking us to Judar, not to some space colony on another planet."

A look of satisfaction chased away the watchfulness in his eyes as he glanced around. "The airport meets your approval?"

"Approval?" Her gaze swept the spread of structures extending as far as her vision reached into the horizon in all directions. "Try stupefaction. This place looks as if it covers all of Judar."

"What you see is the rest of Judar Global Central, Judar's latest and largest project, a Free Zone residential, commercial and manufacturing complex, the biggest and most advanced in the world. The airport is but part of this new community and is the world's largest passenger and cargo hub."

"Tell me about it. This is the first airport I've ever seen with…" She counted. "*Ten* parallel nonintersecting runways."

"It is built for the future, designed to handle all next-generation aircraft. The parallel runways allow up to eight aircrafts to land simultaneously, minimizing in-air queuing. Last year it handled twenty-six million passengers. This year we plan on exceeding the thirty million mark." He tickled Mennah, who was waving around, demanding his attention. "You want me to explain to you, too, *ya sagheerati?* You see those huge glass and steel buildings? Those are four passenger terminals, twelve hotels and I can't remember how many malls. It's lucky we have over two hundred thousand parking spaces, eh? And you see these signs? Each color leads to a transportation linking the airport to Durgham, Judar's capital and your new home, a high-speed freeway, the rail system and the metro."

He turned to Carmen, catching her elbow as her feet wobbled with her first step onto Judarian soil, on a red carpet, no less.

She averted her eyes to the black stretch limo parked at the end of the carpet as his entourage flitted in and out of her field of vision. "It's amazing how everything feels—I don't how to say this—steeped in the stuff of Arabian Nights fables. I don't know how, when everything is so modern, futuristic even. It must be those subtle cultural touches to the designs." She stopped because he did, shifted her feet on the ground, suppressed a shudder. "No, scratch that. It's the land itself."

He looked down at her, the declining sun infusing the gold of his irises with fire, or probably just revealing it. "You feel the land, don't you? It's calling to you. What is it saying?"

It's saying, run now, or you'll never leave. In life or death.

Before she confessed her thoughts out loud, a rumbling separated itself from the airport's background noise, rose to the pitch of approaching thunder.

Caught and held by his probing gaze, she felt no alarm. Probably because he transmitted none, and Mennah seemed to fear nothing in his arms. Carmen interpreted the din only when he released her from his focus, turned it toward the source.

Her reaction still lagged until he said, "Here they are."

It was the pleasure and affection in his voice that made her follow his gaze toward a helicopter the like of which she had never seen, a matte-black majestic alien lifeform.

In seconds it landed a few dozen feet from them in a storm of sound and wind, deafening her, sending her hair rioting, her loose clothes slapping against her flesh. Farooq and Mennah were all smiles as he pointed out the chopper to her, their hair flapping like raven wings. She heard Mennah's screeches of excitement only when the rotors winded down as both doors opened and two bronze colossi descended and started toward them.

Both Farooq's height, one maybe even taller, in body-molding casual chic, one in blacks, one in grays, they looked like the embodiment of the forces of darkness and twilight, modern-day gods descending from the heavens to rule the earth.

And she wasn't being fanciful here. Not by much. She bet they inspired such hyperbole in everyone. She'd bet everyone felt everything holding its breath, slowing down like in movies to emphasize the gravity of their approach.

As the sun slanted golden light and shadows on them, worshipping every sinew of their bodies, every slash of their faces and strand of their hair, it was clear they didn't possess only the same physical blessings and impact as Farooq, but like him they had power and the entitlement of an ancient birthright encoded in their genes. The same genes. Though they resembled him only vaguely, it was unmistakable that they were his blood.

And it was as unmistakable that they were both staring at her, giving her what felt like a total body and mind scan.

She found herself groping for Farooq, this time sagging into him when he contained her in the curve of his body.

As the two men came to a stop at arm's length, they had mercy, terminated their visual and spiritual incursion of only her and instead took in the image of the nuclear family they made.

Did they know how far from the truth this image was?

They had eyes only for Mennah now, who was looking back at them with fascination. And excitement.

A shard of mortification drove in her heart.

Had Mennah's agitation in the presence of strangers been *her* fault? Had she infected her daughter with her own fear, of losing her, transmitted her distrust of everything and everyone? Had she been influencing her into developing neuroses without knowing?

If she had, that was over now. With Farooq's appearance in her life, Mennah had learned fast that she had a defender for life, one with the power to wrestle the world to its knees.

Gray man looked at Farooq before his gaze was dragged back to Mennah. But it was enough. In that moment as obsidian eyes had melded with gold ones, she'd seen a lifetime of understanding, of unbreakable loyalty and unshakable love. Though she'd never had anything like that in her life, she recognized the connection, understood its significance. Even had Farooq not told her about this meeting, she'd have known. This had to be his brother.

Curious about him now she was certain of that, she examined him as he initiated interaction with Mennah, an approach of both eagerness and sensitivity, which the baby responded to wholeheartedly.

He was Farooq's height, with the same daunting proportions, but his face was more symmetrical, his hair a longer sweep down his collar, a rainfall of deepest black with strands kissed by indigo as if manifesting his electric aura, deepening the impact and darkness of his eyes. The eyes of a hypnotist.

He let out a harsh sigh, his rugged face becoming etched with tenderness and wonder as he flicked a finger down Mennah's velvet cheek. *"Ya Ullah, ma ajmalhah."*

Farooq exuded pride and pleasure as Mennah rewarded the ragged comment with a "squee" and a grab of the exploring finger. *"Naffs kalami bed'dubt lamma ra'ait'ha."*

My exact same words when I first saw her.

"Mafi shak, hadi bentak."

No doubt, this is your daughter.

Those words, spoken in a bass voice that was even deeper than Farooq's, brought her eyes to the man in black. She'd been avoiding looking at him. Of the three of them, he unsettled her most.

He was taller than Farooq, maybe by an inch or so, but that wasn't why he overwhelmed her. It was his face, his eyes, what radiated from him, similar to Farooq and the man in gray, but laced with more harshness and danger. The slashed angles and hewn planes of his face were more merciless, the night of his hair total, the trimmed beard deepening the impression of ruthlessness, echoing the desert and its raiders, his eyes that of a lone wolf, hard and unforgiving.

"W'hadi maratak?" he said without looking at her.

And this is your woman?

And she found herself saying, "If you're speaking Arabic to exclude me from this exchange, *I'll* be courteous and tell you it won't work and warn you not to say anything not meant for my ears. According to Farooq, my grasp of Arabic is 'impressive.'"

Four sets of eyes turned to her, three of them boring into her with reactions comparative to each man's character. Farooq's vacillated between that humor he kept losing control over and his intention to add this to her running tab. Gray's was the surprise of someone who couldn't believe he'd mistaken a tigress for a housecat, both amused and intrigued by his faux pas. Black's was unimpressed, his eyes telling her he was quick to judge and impossible to budge. No one got a second chance with him, and she was another false move away from eternal damnation.

But since she was already eyes-deep in it, what the hell.

She shrugged. "I see Farooq has no intention of introducing us. But you know who I am, and, while your identities seem to be need-to-know info he evidently thinks I don't need to know, they're not hard to work out. You must be Shehab and Kamal. And here I have to ask, is this what I should expect from now on?"

Farooq cocked an eyebrow at her. "What is 'this'?"

"This." She swept a gesture from him to Shehab and Kamal. "Are all Aal Masoods like this?"

"Like what?" he persisted.

"Larger-than-life? Description-defying? Will meeting you in your masses be like stumbling into a superhero convention?"

His lips tilted at the corners, his eyes crowding with a cacophony of emotions. She was surprised to feel amusement ruled them all. "Are you flirting with my brothers, Carmen?"

"I'm not even flirting with *you*. I'm stating facts. The three of you are the biggest proof of how grossly unfair life is. Giving you all that must have created severe deficiencies elsewhere. Your personal assets could be divided among three hundred men and they'd still be damn lucky devils."

Gray threw his head back, gave a hearty guffaw. "*B'Ellahi,* I've made up my mind. I like you already, Carmen." She looked at him, unable to hide her gratitude at finding one among the hulks surrounding her who wasn't impossible to reach. He extended a hand to her. Her hand rose automatically, trembled as his closed around it. His smile turned assessing at feeling the tremors arcing through her. He shook her hand slowly, the fathomless black of his eyes brimming with astuteness and good nature. "I'm Shehab. Second son. Kamal is our baby brother."

Said baby brother shot her an implacable look, not following his older brother's example and extending a hand of acceptance.

Gathering the rest of her courage, feeling Farooq's eyes burning the skin off the side of her face, she turned to Kamal. "I'm Carmen. And you don't look like anyone's baby brother."

Was that a hint of surprise in his eyes now? That someone dared breathe, let alone speak her mind, in his presence?

"With two years between me and my 'big' brother, I don't feel like such a baby." Was that a hint of relenting, too?

"So that's why you all look the same age." She cast her gaze between them, shook her head at the magnitude and range of virile beauty displayed before her. "I bet it's great to have siblings so like yourself, so close in age. I would have loved to have any siblings at all, any family—but there you go. I hope you realize how lucky you are to have each other."

The three men exchanged glances, betraying no reaction to her words. She felt it anyway. Surprise. At her words. At their reaction to them. And to her after hearing them.

When they turned their eyes back to her, it felt as if it was with new insight, more interest. She wasn't sure she liked the intensified focus she'd provoked.

She waved between them. "I didn't know you could do that."

"Do what?" Shehab asked, his eyes intent on her.

She wondered at how relative everything was. Seen alone, Shehab would be intimidating. Among his harsher brothers, he was the one who felt kinder, more approachable, the one she gravitated toward, counting on his leniency, his empathy.

She exhaled. "Stand around in the open like that, together."

"You mean Judar's heirs in one sniper's bull's-eye?" A definite shard of lethal humor glinted in the depths of Kamal's eyes. "Though we always take every precaution, it *has* been drilled into us from birth never to put all eggs in one basket, so to speak. Farooq failed to tell us why he made an exception this time."

Farooq shrugged, seemingly no longer concerned with the progress of her first meeting with his siblings, playing with Mennah. "I had to coordinate with you face-to-face. As for the rest, I told you everything there is to know."

Shehab huffed in mockery. "*Aih*, you sure did. I have a daughter," he reproduced Farooq's voice. "Be there when I arrive. I get married tomorrow."

"Tomorrow…?" Carmen choked on the word.

"You didn't get that telegram, eh?" Kamal sounded as if he relished knowing Farooq hadn't put her in the picture, either.

She shook her head, everything getting hazy, the juggernauts surrounding her cutting off air and light and reason. "I got nothing. He only mentioned you to explain your role as witnesses to our—to the-the *orfi* marriage and…and…"

Shehab and Kamal stared at her, no doubt feeling her about to snap with anxiety, then turned to Farooq, eyebrows raised.

Farooq ignored him, his eyes on her, hard with—what? Suspicion? Of what? Her reluctance, her outright panic? Well, surprise. "Do you have any reason for wanting to put off the ceremony?"

"I—I barely set foot here, I need more time…"

"You had sixteen months."

The endlessness of space around them turned into a vise, crushing her. She'd thought she'd have more time…

At that moment, Mennah lurched forward, throwing herself into Carmen's arms. As if she knew how much she needed her, to abort the spiral of agitation, to remind her of why she was doing this.

Shehab, it seemed, thought it time to end the confrontation. He held out his arms to Mennah, who pitched herself at him, as if continuing a game she'd devised of throwing herself around the circle of her new-formed family.

"*Ana amm.*" Shehab held her up, smiles wreathing his face as she wriggled and giggled, performing for her captive audience, pushing her enchantment factor to maximum. "I'm an uncle to this delightful treasure. It's amazing, humbling, and it puts everything in perspective. We're *uncles,* Kamal. Farooq, you're a *father. Ya Ullah,* do you realize what a miracle this is? It's all that matters." He turned on them, holding Mennah out. "She is."

Kamal held out a hand to Mennah, as if unsure whether he could touch her. She grabbed his hand, tried to use it as a chewing toy, before repeating her catch-me maneuver. He caught her, the large hands capable of crushing men trembling, shock and other fierce emotions detonating in his eyes. Pride, protection, possessiveness. He was Farooq's brother, all right.

After a few moments of surrendering to Mennah's pawing, he groaned, "Let's get those marriage papers signed and sealed."

Farooq's face was satisfaction itself at his unyielding brother's capitulation, at how Mennah had secured it without effort. He beckoned, and Hashem materialized carrying the chest.

Farooq took Mennah back from Kamal. Shehab reached for the chest, his eyes on Carmen, as if saying he was on her side. Kamal's eyes, clearing of the emotions Mennah had provoked in him said he'd be watching her, that one step out of line, even if forgiven by Farooq, would guarantee her a formidable enemy for life.

Well, one out of two—make that three—was better than zero.

Farooq pulled her back to him, looked down at her for a moment before he let her have Mennah. "Wait for me in the limo. I'll coordinate tomorrow's ceremony with Shehab and Kamal. Then I'll take you and Mennah home."

Home. They were going home. A home she couldn't even imagine. Farooq's home. Mennah's now. Would it be hers? Could it ever be?

The questions ricocheted inside her until she felt pulped.

She again tried to let the splendor rushing by distract her. It wasn't every day that she drove through a city that had materialized out of revolutionary architects' wildest dreams while retaining its ancient mystery through restored historical sites that blended into the whole, its rawness in preserved natural sights.

No use. She felt no pleasure at the amazing vistas they were sailing through. Thanks to Farooq. He sat at the end of the couch that ran the side of the limo beside Mennah, who was passed out in her car seat, worn-out by her uncles' delight and stimulation, by her newfound extroversion.

"I must know now what you want for your *mahr*."

She lurched. She'd thought he had nothing more to say to her.

He'd always have something to say to her. Something distressing. This time something she'd only heard about, never imagined could ever be applied to her. The *mahr*. The dowry. Paid to the bride in exchange for the right to enjoy marital relations.

She huffed. "Thank you, but I still don't want a sponsor, even a legalized one. A certain amount of 'sharing your privileges' is unavoidable since I'll live with you and Mennah, but that's as far as I'm going, so let's leave it at that."

Imperiousness fired his eyes, tempered by tinges of…what? Humor? Deliberation? Astonishment? She had no idea. "The *mahr* is an obligatory gift from groom to bride. It is your right."

"I can't get my head around the words "obligatory" and "gift" in the same sentence. To my mind they're mutually exclusive."

"Obligations govern relationships, and when observed at their beginnings, they ensure you aren't short-changed or victimized if anything goes wrong. You entered a relationship before observing only the dictates of romantic rubbish, and where did it lead you?"

"Out the other side without owing anyone anything. To freedom with dignity. I wouldn't have it any other way."

He leaned forward, scooped her up, brought her to rest half over him in one move, one of her legs pressing against his hardness. He kept her gaze tethered as he whispered, soft and inescapable, "Name your *mahr*, Carmen."

She lay against him, flayed by his warmth and breath, suffering a widespread neurological malfunction. "I can name anything? You once told me you'd meet any demands I made."

His hand weaved in her hair, his eyes intent on her lips. "Anything. As long as it isn't something unreasonable."

She tried to sit up, felt him expand at her wriggling. "Let's see, what *can* be unreasonable enough for you? How about your fleet of jets? And a hundred million dollar token?"

He ground her harder into his erection. "Done. And done."

This jolted her enough to break the body meld. "Whoa. *So* not done. I was joking. You know the concept, don't you?"

His eyes glowed like slits into an inferno. "I appreciate a slap and tickle as much as the next man, Carmen, but this is no joking matter. Your *mahr* is something only you can estimate, and it is something I'm honor-bound to give you."

She ran her hands through her hair, raised them. "Okay, okay. How about a blinding stone in an obscene size?"

"You will have my mother's betrothal jewelry and whatever you wish of Judar's royal jewels. This is your *shabkah*, not your *mahr*. Shall I consider my fleet and the sum you specified your choice?"

She shot up sitting straight. "You certainly shall not. What would I do with a fleet and a hundred million dollars?"

His pout was cynicism itself. "You want investment advice?"

"Listen, I'm not cut out to be a businesswoman or a shopper, so assets and money would be wasted on me." His eyebrows rose, spoke volumes. She cried, "Does this *mahr* have to be material?"

He threaded his fingers together. "As long as we're alive, yes. When we're ghosts you can have an immaterial one."

"Clever. You know what I mean. Can't it be something...moral?"

"Material things can be quantified. And they last."

"If you think so," she scoffed, "then I feel sorry for you."

"Says the woman who married for 'moral' considerations only to find out how lasting those were. And what would the 'something moral' you want to ask of me be? Love?"

The word, his ridicule as he threw it at her, skewered her. "We agreed that doesn't exist. Or if it does, it doesn't matter."

"Then what do you want?"

She took a deep breath, asked for something as impossible. "A clean slate."

Eight

In a life that had exposed him to betrayals, danger and conspiracies of world-shaking scope, few things ever took Farooq by complete surprise, by storm. If fact, only three things had.

They all involved Carmen.

The way he'd felt when he laid eyes on her. Her telling him she'd had enough of him and walking out. And now, her request.

A clean slate.

She was asking him to surrender his anger, to deny his memory, to erase his knowledge of her crimes. She wanted to start fresh. What for? A way back into his good opinion and goodwill? Into his emotions? Another shot at his faith? Everything she'd once made him lavish on her, and she'd squandered?

The worst part was how she understood him. How she always said or did the perfect thing at the perfect time to have the desired effect on him. His first reaction to her request had been to snatch her in his arms, singe her skin off with the violence of relief, the liberation of capitulation. He still wanted to let his new insight into her ordeals and her exponential effect on him wipe his memory, soothe away the lacerations, drive him to hand her power over him again. He fought the temptation with all he had.

She wasn't here because this was a shiny new beginning and it was her choice to start over, but because he'd given her none. If it had been up to her, no matter her reasons, he would have never found her and Mennah, and Judar would be heading for destruction.

He must never forget that.

But she was flushed with the agitation of hope, while the dread of the little girl who'd grown accustomed to being turned down clouded the heavens of her eyes, made the red-rose petals of her lips tremble, and his convictions evaporated as they formed.

And that was why he couldn't relent.

She'd been destructive as his mistress. As his wife, the mother of his daughter, she'd be devastating. If he let her.

He braced against the pain as he ended this hope for something he wanted as much as she seemed to…more. "Since temporal control to change the past isn't one of my powers, a clean slate is probably the one thing I can't grant you."

It was a good thing he'd given himself that pep talk. Otherwise he would have relented upon seeing her flame dim.

Which was what she probably wanted him to see.

Which he *did* see. That this was no act. That she was scared of her new life, wanted to make peace, wanted a chance. A second chance. And he'd just denied her that.

He bit back a retraction, a promise of all the chances she wanted, if only she'd promise never to lie to him again. Which proved her spell was turning into compulsion. She'd promise anything he wanted. Words were easy.

Or they were supposed to be. The ones with which he fought the thrill her seeming lack of avarice provoked had to be forced to his lips kicking and screaming.

"Since you won't name your *mahr*, I'll use my discretion. And you'll accept it. I'm not having this debate again."

Her flame went out.

Unable to bear the dejection coming off her in waves, he looked out of the window, pretended to ignore her again.

Tomorrow night he'd give her his undivided attention.

Approaching Farooq's palace was like one of those scenes in movies where the heroine nears a boundary that, once crossed, would plunge her into a fairy tale. Or a nightmare.

She was about to cross into one wrapped in the other.

Not that she cared right now. She'd asked for the impossible. He'd pointed that fact out. And she felt…gored.

She knew why she had. Asked. Why she did. Feel this way. Because he made her hope there was a chance it wasn't impossible. A chance to start over, be more than a stray lost in a world she had no place in, clutching a tattered shield of wisecracks and the inconsequence of her dignity.

"Is all this yours?"

The question surprised her. She hadn't intended to ask it.

His eyes turned back to her. "I have my own home, but even if I haven't been living here for the past three years to deal with all that my uncle can't deal with now, we would have come here first anyway. The royal palace is where all royals marry."

This kept getting better. "You mean this is *the* royal palace? And we'll live with the king? And his family?"

His expression filled with mockery. "I assure you your in-laws will not be a source of intrusion. The palatial complex stands on over one hundred hectares, with a three-mile stretch of beach, and its connected annexes boast three hundred twenty rooms and ninety-five suites. And that's not counting the central building housing the royal quarters and halls for royal functions. It will be like living in a hotel compound where you only see other residents with a previous appointment."

"Oh." She couldn't imagine living in the place he'd described, let alone having any role, any say in it. The moment she tried to fine-tune a picture of herself as the crown princess, or the queen overseeing it all, her mind screeched at the enormity of projections, groped for anything to wrench her focus away.

The sights unfolding before her came to the rescue.

Draped in the illumination of a breathtaking sunset, jutting from a peninsula hugged by crystalline waters, the palace crouched like the starship of some giant alien race among many satellites, nestled between expanses of lush landscaped gardens and pristine white beaches, a construction conjured by the highest order of magic, the collaboration of a thousand genies in the era when impossibilities were everyday occurrences, and transported intact through time. She found herself saying all that out loud.

He gave an amused nod. "The forces creating this place were those of hundreds of masters of their trades, from designers to builders to painters to engineers from around the world, who combined faithfulness to Judar's legacy of design and architecture with luxury and state-of-the-art technology. Who needs genies when the magic of imagination and skill can create this?"

"Who indeed."

That was the last thing said as the limo, which she'd long realized was part of a cavalcade, passed through gates ensconced between two towers flying the Judarian flag high above the thirty-foot fence, through street-wide paths lined by palm trees and flower beds and paved in cobblestones. They passed through one tier after another of more gates, courtyards and pavilions until they reached the central grounds of the palace and its extensions.

Everything bore the intricacies and distinctions of the cultures that had melted together to form Judar, the towers leaning toward the Byzantine, the gates toward the Indian, the pavilions the Persian, each twist of metal, each arrangement of stone, every arch and pillar and spire a testimony to one culture's influence or the other, and all ultimately Arabian.

She finally exhaled her admiration. "This place sure gives Buckingham palace and the Taj Mahal a run for their money."

"Since construction was completed five years ago and the royal family moved here from the old palace in Durgham, it has become a national symbol of similar importance, and in this last year has been rising in the ranks of the world's most coveted tourist attractions."

"Tourists are allowed inside?" That was a surprise. She knew how Middle Eastern monarchies guarded their privacy at all costs.

"In certain areas of the palace and its satellites, two days a week, yes. I recommended this to my uncle and he obliged me. Tourism has spiked by three hundred percent since the practice was implemented."

"Wow. That was a great thing to do, Farooq, to give as many people as possible a chance to experience the wonder of this place. To tourists it must feel like walking through an oriental fable."

His smile was tinged with cynicism. "I've heard this is the impression this new palace creates. It doesn't have much to do with reality but that's tourism for you, capitalizing on the notions held by strangers to the land, on the fantasies the culture projects."

Before she could analyze his words, wonder if any pertained to her, the limo stopped. And before she could blink, Farooq grabbed Mennah's car seat, exited the car, then handed her out, too.

And she set foot on the ground of what he'd called her new home.

She stumbled. He kept her up, then had her walking, saved her from looking like a clumsy idiot instead of a self-possessed princess in front of his subjects and employees. He had

her caught up in his body, held up by his power, propelled by
his will. Her pulse escalated until she feared her heart would
either burst or implode. The majesty bombarding her op-
pressed her, its implications in her tiny life unthinkable. Her
breath sheared through her lungs in a mini panic attack as they
walked up the expansive steps of the stone palace, which
soared four towering levels and echoed every hue of the
desert, its roof system sprouting with a hundred domes
covered in mosaic glass and gold finials.

"This place…it's amazing." That wasn't what she'd
intended to say, but a strange excitement was taking over
through her agitation. "I can almost see the grounds and
terraces with the stairs leading down to the beach and marina
lit with strings of lanterns and brass pillars bearing torches,
live *ood* music playing between a blend of accents as head
honchos from around the globe move from one world-shaping
banquet to another."

She turned up entranced eyes, found him staring at her in
the semidarkness, his eyes flaring like burning coals.

Then he exhaled. "Who better than you to see the potential of this place? Regretfully, with my uncle ill for so long,
it has seen no such events in the five years it's been in existence. Our marriage will be the first festive occasion to take
place here."

He fell silent as footmen dressed in ornate uniforms materialized to open the palace's twenty-foot, inlaid-in-gold-
and-silver mahogany double doors. She looked back to catch
its details, then turned to find more wonders to capture her
eyes. The circular columned hall they were crossing had to
be at least two hundred feet in diameter, with a soaring ceiling
at least one hundred feet high, its center sprawling under a
gigantic stained-glass dome.

Her gaze swam around the superbly lit space, got impres-
sions of a sweeping floor plan extending on both sides of the
hall, of pastels and neutrals, of Arabian/Moorish influences

in decor and furnishing, modern ones in finish and feel on a floor spread with polished marble the color of the sand the palace lay on.

Suddenly Farooq said, "Had we had more time, I would have turned over the ceremony to you. Judging by the success you made of the conference you arranged for me, with this place and every power at your disposal, you would have turned it into an event that would have become the stuff of new fables."

His seeming belief in her abilities sent her heart soaring. The images he provoked shot it down, rent and bloodied. Images of the whirlwind of preparations for a life- and world-changing event, the reign of *her* imagination and skills when freed from constrictions of budget and possibilities, of escalating excitement, of jitters of responsibility, of pride of achievement. Of anticipation of ecstasy…

If-onlys cut off her breathing. She stumbled again.

Again he kept her upright, kept talking as if he hadn't crushed her with more futile dreams. "But with my uncle so frail, I wouldn't have gone all-out even if we had the time. It's for the best we didn't."

They entered an elevator that seemed to be an extension of the hall, seemed not to move at all before the doors opened again. Into the past. Into the heart of Arabian Nights.

He tugged her through a huge hall ringed with Arabian-style arches leading to the bowels of a palace within the palace.

The incense fumes rising from mosaic burners hanging from the ceiling hit her compromised balance. He supported her, his touch deepening the dreamscape quality of it all as they passed the central arch through pleated damask drapes woven in rich-earth Berber/Moroccan patterns into a passage lined by sculpted-rock columns. At the base of each, an antique brass lantern blazed, giving the columns' engravings the impact of incantations.

She stared ahead as they approached massive cedar double

doors worked in camel bone and silver that looked as if they'd been transported through millennia intact. They swung soundlessly open with a murmur and a touch from Farooq.

Whoa. Holy voice recognition and fingerprint sensors!

The feeling of stepping centuries both backward and forward in time intensified as they entered another hall with golden light radiating from henna sconces on warm sand-colored walls leading into gigantic living and dining areas interconnected by more arches. Many rooms lay hidden behind closed doors. The whole place, with its enormous proportions, its lavish yet tasteful decorations and furnishings with that incredible ethnic and ultramodern blend, redefined the laws of beauty and luxury.

He led her into one of the living areas. A spherical, intricately fenestrated brass lantern hanging from the ceiling with spectacular chains lit the space. The starry canopy it created showcased the Egyptian mosaic, hand-carved furniture and the plush Moroccan-style couches. It also cascaded over Farooq, adding an unearthly effect to his beauty.

Finding her eyes back on him, he said, "All the things you specified are here. If you need anything else, order it from Ameenah, your head lady-in-waiting. She's Hashem's wife. She'll also get you acquainted with the mechanisms running the place, privacy, security, Internet and entertainment, to mention a few. I'll give her a list of what needs to be done tomorrow. Tonight, relax, take a shower and have an early night. I want you well rested. Tomorrow is the biggest day of your life."

The last sentence rocked her. She turned her swaying into a bend to pick up a hand-woven silk brocade pillow, her tremors into interest over its intricate patterns.

"So these are my and Mennah's quarters?"

He gave her a steady look. "These are my quarters. Ours now. Our bedroom suite is through this passageway." He flicked a hand toward it before indicating the closed doors around them.

"Pick one of these rooms to be Mennah's, where your ladies-in-waiting can tend her when both of us are occupied."

"But I thought…" She couldn't continue, couldn't breathe. Just *couldn't*.

He gave her a serene look. "You thought…what?"

She fought to the surface at his prodding, rasped, "I—I thought I'd have separate quarters."

"And how did you come by that thought?"

Suddenly anger slammed into her. She grabbed at the strength it infused into her limbs, her voice. "I came by it because this isn't a real marriage."

He smiled. As mirthless a smile as those got. "Oh, this is a real marriage. I'd say it's far more real than any you've ever heard about. Notification of our belated marriage ceremony has made it to every embassy. During our flight I received the personal congratulations of every head of state on earth, and though it's on such short-notice, the confirmation of attendance of four major powers' presidents and a dozen kings and queens."

A stunned giggle escaped her. "That's what you call not going all-out? Oh, man…"

"All-out would have been having everyone here for ten days as the royal wedding proceedings unfold. Three days and nights of festivities ending in your henna night, and seven more of palace on national celebrations following the wedding. Having a ceremony after sunset with a banquet for two thousand or so, most of them the entourage of the dignitaries who can't afford not to pay their respects to my king and me in person, *is* keeping it beyond simple. Everyone understands the reasons for that, though, what with us being 'married' already with a child, and with King Zaher not in the best of health."

God. This was too huge. Could he be pulling her leg?

One look into his eyes told her he wasn't. It was probably bigger than her malfunctioning mind could fathom at the moment.

Which gave her hope. "So staying in your quarters is to keep up appearances, right?"

His expression dulled with boredom. "If it pleases you to think that, by all means, go ahead." The boredom evaporated as his pupils engulfed his irises like a black hole would the sun. "But I won't be keeping up appearances and it won't be for an audience's benefit that I'll take you, feast on you, ravish you every night."

Her heart almost fired from her rib cage. "But—but that isn't why we got married."

He inclined his head at her, goading, relishing shredding her nerves. "Why did we get married?"

"Spare me the rhetorical questions, Farooq," she quavered.

"*Zain.* I'll answer them for you. We married for Mennah. And pray tell how did she come into being? Isn't she the living, glorious proof of how much we enjoyed each other's bodies?"

A harsh sound tore open her shutting down lungs. "Sorry to disillusion you but enjoyment doesn't have much to do with conceiving."

"Granted." He moved toward her with the leisure of a cat that had all the time in the world to give his kill a nervous breakdown, putting her out of her misery not even on his mind. "But Mennah's conception *was* a product of absolute pleasure."

She backed away a step for each of his. "That was then."

"And this is now. You dare tell me you don't want me now?"

"I dare all right. Tell you I don't want…this. I don't know what *you* want."

"How can I possibly be more blatant about what I want?"

"You don't want *me.*"

His stare lengthened in the wake of her impassioned cry. Then he picked up her hand, dragged it to him, and this time, he pressed it to his erection. "How do you explain this then?"

She quaked in his hold, her depths gushing in response, unable to muster strength or coordination to snatch her hand away. Not wanting to. Wanting to cup him, map the hardness she wouldn't come close to encompassing, go down on her knees before him, expose him, feel him, taste him, worship him. Only him.

But for him, it wasn't and would never be only her.

The knowledge bled out of her. "You just want sex. Any good-looking woman would do."

"So I'm indiscriminately promiscuous *and* terminally shallow." Before she could define his reaction as mocking or insulted, he went on, his pupils fluctuating, giving his eyes the look of flickering flames. "But if sex with any 'good-looking woman' will do, and we both know I can take my pick of the best-looking who exist, why do I want it with you?"

"Why indeed." And that was a legitimate question. She had no solid theories why he had before, beyond the lure of her total eagerness for him and the why-not factor. Now, she could think of one reason. She said it out loud. "Maybe it's the novelty of a woman you can't have."

"Ah, a challenge to jog my jaded senses." He took the pillow she was holding like a shield, swung it with an effortless flick to the sofa, reached out a hand to her hair, wound a thick lock over and over his fingers, then tugged. Gentle enough not to hurt her, inexorable enough to show her where he wanted her. Against him. He had her there, from breast to calves, his erection pressing into her hip, one leg between hers, rubbing, sawing, until all she wanted was to open them, beg him to end the torment, do all the things he'd threatened, all the things he'd promised. Then his whisper poured into her brain. "I already had you. I have you again. And I'll have you again. And again. And all the time."

She pushed against him, her breath burning, everything shaking out of control. "No. You won't."

He let her go, left her to stumble with the force of her unopposed struggle, smiled at her. "Are you sure about this?"

"I won't let you have me. Not like this."

"Like what? In total hunger, giving you ecstasy?" His certainty, its truth, sent response surging like lava inside her. "Is this what you're objecting to? Too much satisfaction? Maybe you want something a bit…racier, riskier? Maybe some domination, a tinge of danger, of pain? I can oblige you. I probably will, after all this time. I'm not feeling anywhere near gentle. But then, I'm sure you won't want me to be."

She sank deeper in the mire of desire and desperation. "No, Farooq, I don't want this."

The translucency of his eyes fogged, his lips stretching to reveal teeth perfect but for too-sharp canines. "You want nothing more than this. You want nothing *but* this."

She couldn't deny his verdict. But she had to know. "What changed your mind? You were cold, angry…"

His lips remained frozen in that smile that filled her with dread and lust and anticipation. "I'm still cold and angry. It will probably make it all the more explosive."

She raised her hands, an attempt to dilute his convictions, stop her capitulation from being total. "If you think I'm riling you, if you think I can enjoy force…"

He barked a laugh. "Force? The only force I ever used was what I needed to unlock you from around my body."

"That was when there was only goodwill between us, not this—this malice. Don't make it change your mind about the marriage in name only you proposed."

He raised his eyebrows in mock bafflement. "Were we in the same scene back there in your apartment? When did I propose or even imply that 'in name' bit? We were tearing at each other within hours of meeting, and now that we're married, you think it a possibility to keep our hands off each other?"

"We only got married for Mennah." She tried again, desperate to hang on to her separateness, knowing that this time, if she surrendered, there'd be nothing left of her.

"That we married for Mennah, that I would have never married you if not for her, has nothing to do with the fact that I've been burning for sixteen months, needing to feel you underneath me, writhing and screaming your pleasure as I pound into you. No matter how we came to be married, we are. I'm your husband. And I *want* you. You will share my public life as my wife, and you will be my mistress again in private. And I will do everything to you, with you, for you. Everything, Carmen. And then more."

Her legs gave out. She went down like a demolished building, missed the sofa, ended up on the floor leaning on it. She looked up at him, fighting the urge to beg him, if not for the tenderness he'd lavished on her before, then for some assurance what he felt wasn't a cold lust that would consume her to ashes.

"I would have stayed and made you beg for everything you're pretending not to want, but I have to meet my uncle now. I won't be coming back, so you have our bed for yourself for the night. I won't see you again, as is our custom, until the ceremony."

He turned away, strode to the hall. At the connecting arch, he tossed over his shoulder.

"Get all the rest you can. You'll need it."

Nine

Carmen lay on her face on the massage-table, staring at her hands. Her skin had turned into reddish brown lace of extreme intricateness, a different design on each hand. It was as if she was turning into an alien species. A very pretty one, though.

"This is my best *mehndi* henna ever!" Ameenah exclaimed, marveling at her handiwork. She raised shining black eyes to Carmen, her smile displaying her lovely teeth and nature, deepening her dark beauty. "But then it's your input that turned it into a masterpiece. It is ingenious, how you designed those patterns made of *somow'el Ameer* Farooq's name in all the languages you know."

Yeah. She'd gone all-out, to borrow a word of his.

Ameenah rose from her kneeling position before her. "I so hope he'll decipher your homage without being told."

Carmen only smiled. *She* was hoping he wouldn't notice.

Writing his name all over her body was something she'd done for herself, on an unstoppable impulse, as if she'd feel closer to him this way, say all the things she couldn't and had never been able to say out loud, make all the confessions he had no use for.

She rose, put on her clothes, marveling at how she'd been able to strip almost naked in Ameenah's presence to get her henna done. Just like her husband, Ameenah made her, and Mennah, feel they'd known her forever, could depend on her. She already had in so many things during the day. Her wedding day.

After Farooq left her last night, she was too agitated to do anything, let alone sleep. But Ameenah breezed in, all smiles and welcome, bearing the list Farooq had given her to perform on Carmen in preparation for the wedding. And the wedding night.

After her first pensiveness and reluctance, Ameenah's cheerfulness and enthusiasm infected her, made everything feel so much better, even fun.

She threw herself into the spirit of things, surrendered to Ameenah's mastery of coddling as she carried out her crown prince's directives. With the help of Salmah and Hend, her daughters, she sorted through her things for Carmen, got her acquainted with the mind-boggling facilities in the palace. Then, while Carmen fed Mennah dinner and answered e-mails, they went out, returned with a rack of clothes from which to choose a wedding outfit.

She'd known this was coming. She should have been surprised at the range and lavishness of the outfits and nothing more.

She did more. She burst into tears. She, who'd never shed a tear even when her mother had died, who hadn't known what crying was until after she'd left Farooq. But she'd never thought she'd wear a wedding dress again, and for it to be something of this caliber, in which to marry Farooq…

The good part was the ladies were totally sympathetic. More, it seemed she won their hearts by displaying such human frailty, such emotional involvement. Ameenah let her know it was only fitting that Farooq married a woman who so deeply recognized the blessing of marrying him, who worshipped him as he deserved to be worshipped.

At the sight of the clothes, Mennah crawled at top speed, hurled herself among them, yelling in excitement at the feel of the rich layers of cloth, at the colors, no doubt recognizing the sheer decadence of each creation. She tried to chew and taste her favorites and, clever baby that she was, the one she chewed hardest was the one Carmen felt had been created for her.

An incredible burnt red-orange the exact color of her hair three-piece Pakistani/Indian/Arabian-design creation, it had a *jamawar* silk corset top with wide shoulder straps and a concealed zip closure at the back. It was scalloped on all edges, more elaborate at a décolleté that dipped just above her cleavage. It was heavily hand-embroidered with intricate floral designs of silver and gold thread and embellished in sequins, beads, pearls, crystals, semiprecious stones and appliqué in every shade of turquoise, azure and sky-blue, all the shades of her eyes. It had echoing armbands that rained gold beaded tassels, with matching chiffon veils attached that cascaded to her hands.

The skirt was a trailing *lehenga* of turquoise chiffon over shimmering azure silk taffeta lining, its embroidery and embellishments echoing the top's, in coral, ruby and garnet shades with scalloping at the hemline. The third piece was a veil *dupatta* in dual shading of coral/crystal-blue with scalloped, heavily embellished borders and vivid azure edging on the corners.

When Ameenah moved to the next item on the list, adjusting it to fit her, Carmen threw herself into the pleasure of handling such exquisiteness, letting her sewing skills loose. Among them they turned it into a custom-made creation in under an hour. The enjoyment lasted until it was time for the next item on the list.

Choosing the accessories.

From Farooq's mother's jewelry. And Judar's royal jewels.

Ameenah and half a dozen guards escorted Carmen to a gigantic vault deep underneath the palace. As she stepped inside, she knew how Ali Baba had felt on entering the cave of the forty thieves.

Beyond dazzled at the treasure she thought reason enough to have an invasion mounted on the palace, on Judar, she hesitantly chose a set matching her outfit's colors. She wouldn't have been able to choose based on anything else. It was a twenty-four-karat gold-lace Indian-style choker with a design undulating to a central pendant reaching below her collarbone, matching shoulder-length earrings, bracelet and anklet. All pieces were inlaid in aquamarines, sapphires and rubies, with eight-point star motifs with a diamond center, one karat each in the necklace and a ten-karat stone in the pendant.

She still wanted to be reassured that Farooq had been serious when he'd said she could wear them. Ameenah insisted she *owned* them.

And she panicked. "Who'd want to possess something that needs to be kept in a vault and guarded by an army round the clock?"

"Now you are the crown prince's wife," Ameenah said sagely. "Without a stitch of possessions, you're worth far more, would be ransomed for a hundred times the royal jewels' worth."

Carmen was stunned that she hadn't realized this before. "God, you're right. I'm still thinking as an ordinary person, thinking how vulnerable I'd be if people knew I possessed something of that value. But we're not ordinary anymore. Mennah and I have become two of the most coveted targets in the world."

"This is true of every member of the royal family," Ameenah soothed. "But it's a potential that has never come to pass. And it will never be a consideration for *somow'ek or somow'el Ameerah* Mennah. Beyond the invisible protection *Maolai Walai'el Ahd* will provide for you, no criminal or power in the world would touch a hair on your heads anyway. No one would risk his wrath. Or that of *somow'wohom,* Shehab and Kamal."

She conceded that, her alarm subsiding. No one would be stupid enough to piss off any of those all-for-one-and-one-for-all men at all, let alone that much.

On returning to Farooq's apartments, Carmen took a bath with Mennah in one of the magnificent bathrooms spread with marble and gold, then collapsed into a bed by Mennah's crib. She woke up eight hours later and Ameenah started the henna even as Carmen and Mennah had breakfast, to give it time to dry and stain.

Ameenah wasn't happy that the color wouldn't ripen to its deepest for the ceremony or even for the wedding night, but said, "There's tomorrow night, and the night after, then a lifetime of joy in your husband-and-prince's arms, as he enjoys you and your efforts to make yourself beautiful for him and pleasures you in turn."

Carmen simulated a smile for the kind woman. Even if she could confide in her, she wouldn't burden her with her despondency. Whatever awaited her with Farooq wasn't a lifetime of anything. She probably had until he was sated and avenged. There was no point in projecting how soon that would be.

As he'd said to her two days ago, there wasn't a choice here…

Mennah scampered off the sofa, wrenching Carmen to the present, and dashed toward the polished brass tray table laden with multicolored, hand-painted-in-gold tea glasses.

To her baby's chagrin, Carmen intercepted her, scooped her up, turned to Ameenah. "Okay, I'd say its time to bring in your team."

They were coming to childproof the living quarters, and to make adjustments to the bedroom suite per Farooq's instructions.

She hadn't spent the night there. She'd only taken a look inside. The sparsely furnished suite was as big as the whole apartment outside, with soaring domed ceiling, ringed by the same Arabian-style columns and arches, permeated by an over-powering male influence in every brushstroke and article. His.

She wondered about the "adjustments" he'd ordered. The place looked perfect as is. But she wouldn't be around to see them being installed, being busy starting the dressing up procedure.

She'd see them soon enough, though.

The wedding was in two hours.

She looked down at Mennah who was looking longingly at the glasses, lips drooping at the corners. "Don't be sad, darling. Everything I do is to keep you safe and happy. It's all for you."

"It's time, *ya Ameerati.*"

Carmen started. She'd known Ameenah would say that. It still jolted her. Time. It was time.

She was marrying Farooq. A real marriage. At least, real in form, in the physical side. It wasn't permanent, but who ever entered marriage positive it would last? People only assumed, *hoped* it would. It made no difference that she was entering theirs ahead in the game, without assumptions, without hope, knowing it wouldn't. She'd decided to make the best of it. While it lasted.

She was marrying him in a ceremony attended by the king of Judar, by world leaders. And she wasn't just some jittery, out-of-place, over-her-head waif.

Well, okay, she was. But that was only a part of her. The personal part, the one no one had to know about. She had more components to her. She was also the mother of Judar's princess. And she was a highly skilled professional, armed with every ability and knowledge to handle such a situation. In fact, it felt as if everything she'd learned and practiced in life had been pre-paring her for this moment, this event. As he'd said, who better than her? To navigate the rapids of an international gathering, bridge differences, meet disparate expectations?

No one, that was who.

She *would* honor Mennah, and her new position.

She would honor him.

Closing mind and ears to anything but this high note of her self-addressed pep talk, she walked out.

Ameenah walked behind her, resplendent in her bridal matron gown, carrying Mennah who looked heartbreakingly cute in a getup made in haste to match her mother's. Ameenah's daughters followed, heading the procession of her ladies-in-waiting, all stunning with their glowing olive complexion and their dark hair streaming down their backs, their lithe bodies wrapped in exquisite sarilike dresses in azures and golds that complemented her gown.

The wedding was taking place in the southern gardens, where the desert and sea winds remained calm as the night deepened. She'd been informed that Farooq would be waiting for her at the southern entrance to escort her to where the *ma'zoon* would write *el ketaab,* their public marriage certificate. She'd chosen not to have a proxy, to perform the rituals herself. Shehab and Kamal were the two required witnesses again…

Agitation and anticipation congealed. Air, the world, disappeared. *Farooq.*

He was standing at the wide-open doors. Waiting for her. He was obscured by distance, by shadows. But she saw him, felt him with everything in her. And all she wanted was to run to him, throw herself in his arms, tell him, show him, beg him…

Thunder assailed her the moment she descended the last step. The *zaffah,* the traditional bridal procession, a unique, instantly recognizable rhythm belted out on *doffoof,* huge tambourinelike instruments, for two bars before singers joined in, chanting the praises of the bride, congratulating her on her magnificent groom and wishing her eternal happiness. And bountiful progeny.

She managed not to falter, and after making sure the blaring beat hadn't startled Mennah, she kept walking, head held high, with quick, purposeful steps toward Farooq, who stood with his feet planted apart, his hands linked, waiting for her to have her *zaffah*, to come give him herself. As she couldn't wait to do.

When only two-dozen feet remained, he moved out of the shadows. Her heart stopped.

No deceleration, no warning. It just stopped.

And she no longer needed it to beat, to push blood to her brain, to keep her legs moving. They moved on their own, powered by everything about him that demanded her, at once. Her vision didn't dim. It remained clear and riveted on him.

If she'd thought he'd looked indescribable before, in suits, in any clothes, out of them, Farooq in traditional royal groom costume showed her what a loss for words, for *thoughts*, really meant.

All she could think was, he was dressed in blues and muted golds shades darker than those in her outfit. He matched her so much, she had to believe he'd done so on purpose.

Her agitation and pleasure sharpened to pain as she devoured every nuance of the heavy silk *abaya* as it hugged his shoulders, cascaded to his ankles, emphasizing his breadth and height. Its edges, shoulders and cuffs were heavily embroidered in gold and bronze thread and sequins in a paisley cashmere pattern. Underneath it, a striped top in the same colors buttoned down from his Adam's apple, stretched across his chest, crisscrossed by bronze metal belts. Another six-inch belt spanned his waist, anchoring ceremonial curved dagger and sword sheathed in gold scabbards over bronze pantaloons whose looseness hid none of the potency beneath.

This was Farooq as he really was, the heir to a legacy rooted in fables, a shaper of destiny, the embodiment of the desert and the sea, the incarnation of their might and wealth, their majesty and beauty.

And he was her groom, the man who'd given her what had made life real—the agony of loving him—and what had made it worth living, her miraculous Mennah. He was the man she still loved beyond sanity or hope.

He stood there, his eyes branding her as his. As she was, had been from the first moment.

Her heart had restarted at some point, propelling her toward him faster with each beat. His hand rose, asking for hers. She ran the last few steps, flew, both hands held out, grabbed his as if afraid he'd fade away.

"Carmen." She heard his rumble over the din, felt it in her bones, his astonishment, his possessiveness, his hunger as he crushed her hands in the assuagement of his reality.

Needing more proof, she burrowed into his side. His arm convulsed around her as the other ended the *zaffah* with a wave. He looked down at her, bombarding her with ferocity. She buried her face into his chest, seeking refuge from him in him.

His heart, his groan thundered below her ear. "Let's get this done before I give in, Carmen."

Without giving her time to wonder what he meant, he had her striding beside him on the royal-blue carpet, down the expansive path lined with stunning plant and flower arrangements ending in a dozen cream satin-covered steps. They climbed up to the *kooshah,* where bride and groom sit during the ceremony. Theirs was a massive gazebolike structure with clusters of exquisite Arabesque woodwork hanging from its eight corners like pendent stalactites, gilded on the outside, the color of cedar on the inside. Within its pillars was a huge curved cream-satin couch ensconcing an antique worked bronze table. The *ma'zoon* sat in the middle with their *orfi* marriage scrolls in front of him, and a book that looked like some ancient tome of prophecy open to empty pages where their destiny was still to be written.

The live music came to an end as Farooq led her to the edge of the stage and all her resolutions to be the seasoned professional boiled away. Being the designing mind behind such events was realms away from literally being centerstage in one.

Her arrhythmia somehow didn't shake her apart as she cast her gaze around the expansive gardens, even when it took a further plunge into irregularity. The gardens were decorated in the exact way she'd imagined and told Farooq about yesterday. Hundreds of lanterns undulated in the twilight breeze between symmetrically planted palm trees. Hundreds of torches flamed on top of polished brass poles, all intertwined between two hundred tables set in a level of luxury she'd only ever dreamed of achieving in her own enterprises, occupied by people who made the world go 'round.

And they were all looking at her. In resounding silence.

Her hand squeezed Farooq's. He squeezed back, leaned to put his lips to her ear. "Your beauty has stunned them, *ya jameelati.*"

Breath left her. Not at his assertion, as touched as she was by it, but at his endearment. Not because it was "my beauty," but because she'd given up on hearing one from his lips again. It was like gulping crisp water after months in the desert.

Then he murmured, "Let's work the crowd, *ya helweti.*"

Elation at yet another endearment, *my sweet,* bubbled over. She smiled with all her body, surged forward with him to wave to the attendees, who'd all stood up and started clapping.

Smiling wide, he winked. "Now let's play our trump card."

He turned and Ameenah came forward with Mennah, who launched herself into his arms. He held her up, showing her off, pride and love radiating from him. The crowd succumbed in collective to Mennah's cuteness and excitement, awing at the sight of her, chuckling at Farooq's intentional Lion King reference. Their clapping rose when he handed Mennah back to Carmen and bowed before her, branding her hand on both sides in kisses.

As he withdrew his lips, straightened, her heart stuttered, felt it would stop again, for real, if she lost contact with him.

She surged to maintain it, threw herself at him, Mennah and all. He went rigid. Silence descended.

She closed her eyes. *Oh* God. Way to be a professional

limpet. Had she deepened his anger at her? Did all those people who mattered to him and to Judar on so many levels think the crown prince had settled on an impulsive moron for a wife, casting doubts on his judgment, damaging his image…?

Agitation came to an abrupt end as Farooq swept her, Mennah and all, high in his arms. The crowd roared with approval.

Sagging in his hold in relief, she opened her eyes, sought his, found them roiling with hunger and delight.

"If you're trying to make your bill too huge to pay, you've only succeeded in enlarging the installments I'll exact from you. But now you have to cater to all those poor power brokers whose jaded senses you've jogged. They're clamoring for more."

He let her feet touch ground, gave her a slight push. He wanted her to go salute their guests alone, the so-called estranged princess laying claim to her rightful status.

Holding the waving Mennah tighter in her arms, she let her fingers and gaze trail off his, started across the stage, an out-of-body feeling coming over her. It was as if she was in the crowd watching that confident woman in the thousands of dollars outfit and priceless jewelry waving and smiling to the people who shaped and ruled earth as if she was one of them.

In the first row she recognized oil, shipping, and technology magnates. The German chancellor. The French president. The king and queen of Bidalya. And…was that the king of Judar…?

Sick electricity arced from her armpits, flooding her body. He looked so unwell, she almost hadn't recognized him. And he didn't look happy. Displeasure came off him in waves. There was no question in her mind. *He didn't want Farooq to marry her.*

Was Farooq going against his king's wishes? Or had the king given his consent on terms of it being a finite union? How finite?

And why was she wondering? She'd already known her days with Farooq were numbered. Again. Had she been fooling herself into thinking they might not be? Where had she learned that mutilating practice? When had she learned to hope?

A blacker wave of unease crashed into her. She traced its source to a man she'd seen only once. Tareq.

He'd seemed to suck up positive energy then, too, but she'd thought her condition when she'd stumbled into him during her life's darkest hour had imparted its oppression and grimness on him. It had seemed the only logical explanation when the man had gone out of his way to be accommodating when he'd found her staggering out of Farooq's skyscraper that night, weeping and lost. He hadn't probed when she'd said she needed to get away, had done all he could to help her. She'd never thought about why he had.

Now she felt his maliciousness focus on her, on Farooq, and she knew. He'd hoped it would hurt Farooq, or at least anger him greatly.

Insight became conviction. He'd introduced himself as Farooq's older cousin. That was why she'd accepted his offer of a ride. But that meant *he* must have been the first in line to the throne. And he'd been bypassed for Farooq. He Farooq's his enemy. He hated him, would do anything to hurt him. Would he go as far as physical harm…?

Suddenly she was suffocating with dread and hatred.

Farooq took Mennah from her, handed her back to Ameenah, and reached for her frozen-in-sweat hand, stilled its shaking. She found his gaze fixed on Tareq, his face turned to stone as he met his cousin's menace.

"Farooq…" She wanted to beg for reassurance, that he was safe, that Mennah was as he turned her to the *kooshah*, where Shehab and Kamal flanked the couch, in full traditional regalia. She caught their eyes, hers begging, for some reason believing they'd understand her fears, defuse them. They cast their gazes behind her, she just knew at Tareq. Then Shehab gave her a reinforcing glance, Kamal a ferocious one, as if each was telling her in his way not to worry.

Farooq's gaze was once more inscrutable as he seated her on one side of the *ma'zoon* before sitting on the other.

"Carmen, give me your hand," Farooq said, starting the ritual of *katb ek-ketaab*, literally writing the book, of matrimony. They'd hold hands, oppose thumbs, and the *ma'zoon* would place a pristine piece of cloth over their hands, place his on top and recite the marriage vows for each to repeat after him.

Overcome, by emotion, by everything, she gave him her hand.

Farooq stared at Carmen's hand. Was that...?

It was. His name. She'd written his name on her hand. And wait...that was his name, too. There. And there. It was everywhere. All over her hands. In Arabic and the other languages she spoke. He'd bet that Chinese script was it, too. Written in a way as to be the building blocks of the exquisite patterns, and to be almost indecipherable. He saw it right away.

It wasn't a custom here to kiss the bride. He'd make it one. He'd make kissing the bride within an inch of her life the new rage. He'd end up hauling her over his shoulder and giving the international assembly a reason to think Judar would one day have a king who would revert it to the days of desert raiders.

Everyone should be grateful he was suffering through the motions at all. The moment he'd seen her descending those stairs, with that distressing outfit hugging her lushness, constricting her waist, echoing her magnificent colors, intensifying them, he'd wanted to charge her, lug her back to their quarters, end the waiting and to hell with everything.

He would have done it and thought of his king and other guests only after he'd taken the edge off the hunger enough to regain coherence. Then she'd tampered with his desire further, as always doing the last thing he'd expected. She'd *run* to him.

Ya Ullah, she'd run, as if she was his old Carmen, as if he was everything she had or could ever want. She'd groped for his hand, cleaved to his side like a vital part of him that had been hacked out and then restored.

And now her hands. Those hands that had once weaved spells and wrung sanity from him were doing so again with the incantation of his name in all the tongues she commanded, in an unprecedented confession. As her offer of herself, her every act of generosity had once done.

This was no plea for a clean slate. This was a command for carte blanche. One he wanted to obey with everything in him. Especially now that his king had succumbed to Tareq's insistence on attending the ceremony and he'd seen how she'd looked at him.

Her reaction had been unmistakable. Revulsion. Dread.

Had Tareq been blackmailing her? Threatening her? This was a new motive he hadn't thought of before. One that would make her a victim rather than an accomplice. Dare he believe it? That this time she had no ulterior motive? That she'd always been coerced, that the only truth had been her desire for him?

The jewels of Carmen's eyes corroborated her hands' silent confession. Fanned the flames of hunger. And of hope…?

No. He hoped for nothing. But he hungered for everything.

He nodded to the *ma'zoon,* watched him place the monogrammed House of Aal Masood handkerchief over their hands, hers bearing her passive weapon of mass destruction, heard him clear his throat.

"*Somow'el Ameerah* Carmen, repeat after me…"

It was done. And he was trapped.

At his king's side. In the mire of protocol. Unable to roar to everyone that they'd done their bid for foreign policy, and to go away now so he could ravish his bride.

The bride who, besides entrancing the crowd en masse before proceeding to entrench her effect one-on-one, was in the advance stages of wrapping his king around her finger. The king who'd told him last night what a time bomb he considered her.

Having Carmen now was a necessary evil, he'd said, to

secure the succession, but didn't Farooq realize that, as a woman not of their culture and creed, she might be the lit fuse to set off the volatile mess Judar was mired in?

Then, ten minutes in her company and she'd had him laughing as he hadn't laughed in years. Two hours later, as they'd made the rounds of all the heads of state, he was showing her off as if she were one of his daughters.

Farooq had given Carmen two more hours to work her magic on the crowd, bringing poles together, riding the currents of the rife-with-potential-pitfalls situation, milking it for all the boons it could yield. In testimony to her effect, after talking to her at length in his mother tongue, an Argentinean magnate who'd formerly decided not to set his next worth billions IT project on Judarian soil had approached Farooq with his change of heart.

But even if she'd manage to negotiate an end to major conflicts if she circulated longer, he wasn't waiting one more second. He turned on the mike clipped to his *abaya*'s collar.

"My king, venerable guests…" Everyone turned to him. "I thank you for the honor of your presence and the generosity of your blessings. I hope you'll continue to enjoy yourselves longer, but I have an urgent matter to attend to…" He dragged Carmen to him, stabbed his fingers into her garnet waterfall beneath its flowing veil, crashed his lips down on hers. He invaded her, consumed her in the kiss he'd been depriving himself of, the one he intended to go down in history. He reeled with her reaction, taste, feel, with the incongruity of hearing hoots from such a congregation. Those people welcomed the spontaneity for once, didn't they? He kicked to the surface with all he had, swept the half-fainting Carmen up in his arms. "I'm sure you'll all see the pressing urgency of putting my estranged wife where she belongs. Back in my bed."

Ten

Carmen felt no heavier than Mennah, felt airborne, invincible, felt cherished and craved, and everything that wasn't real all the way to Farooq's quarters.

Or were they? She'd been lost in the tumult of marveling at his beauty as he swept through the palace, in the single-mindedness of his intentions and the way he'd announced them to everyone. Now she was no longer sure where he'd taken her. The sleeping quarters she'd seen this morning had been the utilitarian space of a man who had few needs and not much time for luxuries. This place was a cross between a sultan's chambers of erotic decadence and a bridal suite from another reality.

But it was the same place, if only judging by its structure. Not one piece of the furniture she'd seen remained. On the right wing was a sitting area of wine-red couches over acres of handwoven silk Persian carpets of complementing colors. On the left was a dining area for two with a polished hand-carved mahogany round table set with an incredible dinner. Separating the wings, from previously bare ceilings rained cascades of extensively pleated, cream-colored voile drapes that caught and suffused the lights from hundreds of candles burning at the base of each of the arabesque columns ringing the huge space. Sweet-spicy *ood* incense burned in urns below the arches, its fumes swirling up in the blazing candlelight like scented ghosts. In the background, evocative recorded music droned, on an instrument also called ood, Spanish guitarlike but with more exotic intonations, adding to the mystic lasciviousness that permeated the place.

Farooq crossed the intricate woodwork floor toward a square bed that spread below the dome, surrounded on two sides by drapes, with a gigantic mirror in a gilded, elaborately carved frame as headboard. It was the largest, thickest mattress she'd ever seen, layered in cream and white sheets, looking like a huge *mille-feuille,* with the last layer the frosting of a cream lace cover. Dozens of colorful pillows of all sizes were scattered all over it and around it, like fruits surrounding an indulgence.

She tried to cling to him, bring him down with her, on her, as he placed her on it. He pulled back. Her arms fell away, stinging with the need to be filled with his bulk, with the letdown. He circled the bed, then did something that sent her heartbeats scattering. He mounted it, stood there at its far end. Just stared at her. She couldn't take it, held out her arms again, begging for him, risking another rebuff.

It was as if a switch was hit, pushing everything inside him to maximum, the intensity emanating from him marrow-jarring.

Yet he still didn't move, stood there, containing it all, his body clenched with the effort, examining her abandoned pose.

He waited until she lowered her arms, her hands fisting on the hollow pain inside her chest, before he drawled, "What changed your mind, to borrow a question of yours?"

He meant about wanting him. She told him the truth, as she would from now on. "I haven't. I never said I don't want you."

His jaw tightened. "I remember statements to that effect."

"I only lied to you about that once, Farooq. Anything I said or implied since then was because it seemed best not to complicate matters by bringing up what I thought you no longer wanted from me."

"So you want me." She came up on one shaking elbow, reached out a hand in confession, in supplication. "No. I must have more than silent invitation and surrender. More than my name all over your hands. Say it, Carmen. I must have the words. The words you once lavished on me."

And she gave them to him. "I wanted you from the moment I saw you. I never knew there was wanting like that, that I was equipped to feel something so fierce, so total. I never stopped, and I can never stop craving you, Farooq. God knows how hard I tried. Whatever I said since we met again was me trying to spare myself pain and humiliation."

His pupils, his whole body expanded in affront. "You're saying I hurt and humiliated you?"

"*No,*" she cried out. "You only ever gave me every satisfaction and consideration. Even when you found me again and had every reason to feel betrayed and insulted, to exact punishment, you still treated me with restraint, gave me rights another man would have considered forfeit. You even wanted to give me much more than I could ever accept. I wasn't protecting myself from you. I realize now I never feared you. I feared circumstances, reality, your complex status and existence, my own hang-ups. But I knew I would be injured anyway. I couldn't afford to get hurt when I must be the mother Mennah needs and deserves."

His teeth scraped together, his nostrils flaring. "So again I ask, what changed your mind?"

"Everything sank in," she said, coming to terms with her

own feelings and decisions. "The depth of your feelings and commitment to Mennah. Then last night I realized you still want me, and not just as Mennah's attachment, as you at first made it sound."

The ood trilling in the background launched into a haunting passage, as if scoring her words, underscoring the silence that expanded between them in their wake.

Still standing there like another wonder from the hyper-reality of this place, a colossus carved by gods of virility, he said, "Do you remember the night you walked out on me?"

"God, don't…"

He cut across her plea. "Do you remember what I said?"

She fisted her hands on the lace cover trying to alleviate the stinging that felt like her nerves had turned into hot needles, all trying to burst out of her skin.

"I remember what *I* said," she moaned. "Do you know how many times I wanted to take it back? Every moment I was myself, and not the single, working mother, that's how many times. Every time I imagined how I would explain my behavior then, how you trapped me when you wouldn't let me walk away without explanations, that I considered pretending to take your offer, pretend that had been my objective, but couldn't do that to you. Not after you gave me a glimpse into what being *you* means, what kind of segregation and alienation you live in, unable to trust anyone's feelings and intentions toward you…"

Something burst out of him, too furious and abrasive to be a laugh. "So you thought it better to let me think you were a promiscuous wretch than a mercenary bitch? You decided to stab my emotions as a man, my ego as a male, rather than consolidate my paranoia as a prince? Only you could think of something like that."

"At least I retained part of the truth," she quavered. "That my desire was real and for you, not what you can provide."

His hands fisted. "While it lasted, you mean."

So he still wanted more…assurance? No. That implied emotional involvement, and none of this had been about that on his side.

But…he'd said she'd "stabbed his emotions as a man." Did that mean…?

No. *No.* Don't even go there. Don't even think it.

But the way he'd said it all… "You talk as if you bought my act, when the first thing you said was that you saw through it."

"You keep putting the weirdest things in my mouth. When did I ever say anything to that effect?"

"You kept saying things like 'save it,' 'more acts' and commenting on my acting abilities."

"The act I was referring to was that of the unbridled lover who couldn't get enough of me. Now you tell me *that* was the truth. The only truth. I believed you the first time, every word, every touch instantly and completely. This time, I'm in need of proof."

And she wanted to give it to him, wanted to give him everything in her. If he wanted it. It didn't matter for how long.

She held out her arms to him again, shaking with the enormity of her love, the jump she was taking, the depths she was exposing. "Make your demands, Farooq. I'll meet them. Whatever they are."

He bared his teeth on a silent growl, his body tensing as if at the shock of a lash. Did her offer, the echo of his all those months ago, in words if not in meaning, hit him that hard? Because she was matching his material offers with the one thing she owned, could give, herself? Did he even want that much of her?

He still wouldn't move, his eyes becoming almost scary in their focus. "I asked if you remember what I said. Not what I said after your dropped your bomb. What I said when I came in. That I was almost afraid to touch you, that I thought it would take us to the edge of survival, after two days of deprivation." She lurched under the power of memory, the potential of reality. He started to move then, in steps laden with the danger of ebbing control, of near-explosion fierceness. "Use that insight of yours and picture how I feel now, what it will be like, after sixteen months."

Her senses ricocheted within a body that felt hollow. Every breath, every tremor, electrocuted her. Every heartbeat felt like a wrecking ball inside her chest. He kept coming, cruel in his slowness, blatant in his intentions.

"I don't need to picture anything," she gasped. "It's been tearing at me all that time, it's tearing me apart now. Please, Farooq, show me what the edge of survival feels like…"

He gave a rumble that traveled through the mattress then through her, made her feel she was lying on a livewire. Still rumbling, he stopped above her, looking at her like a lion deciding which part of his prey he'd devour first. Then he started to undress. The sheer injustice overcame her enervation, sent her surging up to snatch the privilege for herself.

He held out a warning finger. "Don't touch me, Carmen. It is no exaggeration, what I just said."

The one thing that made her abide by his admonition was realizing he wasn't undressing. He was just removing his ceremonial dagger and sword, his metal belts, like a warrior back from battle, relinquishing the evidence of one form of savagery, his eyes promising her another.

Throwing everything to the end of the bed, he kneeled beside her, let his hands hover over her, like that night, mimicking in pantomime all he'd do to her, all the liberties he'd take. Then he bent over her, his lips tormenting a flight pattern of their own.

And he told her. "I couldn't touch you for real, couldn't kiss you when we were alone. I had to remain distant, until I came to grips with the violence of my craving for you. But I can't. I never lose control. Unless it's you."

This was everything she could dream of, would risk everything for. *Her* Farooq back, confessing the depth of his desire.

Disregarding his warning, she lunged for him, hands trembling on the fastening of his pantaloons, the thousand buttons keeping his flesh away from her greed.

His growls detailed his enjoyment of her frenzy even as he ended it, grabbed her, flipped her on her stomach. Then he straddled her hips. She raised her head, met their images in the mirror headboard. He raised his eyes, meeting hers in the reflection. Instead of imparting a measure of detachment, the replicas moving in the coolness of glass sent her blood seething in her veins.

She cried out, arched her hips up, seeking more contact with him. He pushed her down, one hand flat on her back, his hardness digging into her buttocks, before he moved her again until she was lying sideways to the mirror, for a full-body view. He lay on top of her, keeping her eyes captive, grinding into her, mimicking what she was longing for him to do without the chafing barriers. Then he reared up, slowly unclipped the veil from her hair.

"I never liked red hair. But this…" He threaded his hands into it, raised the locks, let them fall. "This texture, this wave, this hue, that it's on top of *this* head…" His fingers dug into her scalp, massaged, had her thrashing beneath him. He suddenly bunched her locks, pulled on them as if they were reins.

She arched back, lips opening on the sharpness of stimulation, panting for his. He slammed into her buttocks, gave her a hand to kiss, to bite into, before he pushed her down again.

"Do you know what seeing you in that outfit did to me?" He began to unzip her corset top. Then he stopped. She saw his face seize in the mirror. She twisted around to get the reality, saw his raptness focused on the henna patterns on her back, felt his renewed rumbling forking through her. And he hadn't even seen their extent yet. Next moment the rumbling quaking her bones intensified as his fingers traced the spots where the patterns made up of his name clustered. He'd deciphered her homage.

She was elated now that he had. She should be alarmed that

she was tampering with the control of a being of such destructive potential, but she wasn't. He'd never lose control. Not that way. Not her Farooq. But he *was* losing his distance, his separateness to her power over him, to the sight of his name emblazoned all over her body. That was one of two things she wanted from life.

He flipped her onto her back, gloriously rough, dragging her top down to her waist, spilling her breasts into the palms they'd been made to fill, kneading them with a careful savagery that had her bucking beneath him. Her hands flailed, trying to tear his top open, needing the crush of his chest. He grasped both her hands in one of his, the other holding his top at the neck and shredding down. He tore off his *abaya,* pushed his tattered top wider, exposing the magnificent sculpture of his torso. She keened as her salivary glands stung. She needed her lips and tongue on his flesh, her teeth in it.

"There are more places I want my name on." He slid down her body, the silk of his body hair brushing her every inch into a distress of arousal. "Here." He gently bit each nipple in turn, had her crying out, before settling into a ruthless rhythm of suckling that had magma pouring from her core, until she was pummeling him for the release only the power of his possession would grant her.

He caught her clawing hands, slammed them to the bed in one of his, slid down as he bunched her *lehenga* up and her thong down to her feet. "And here…" He let go of her hands, held her feet apart, alternated kisses between them, suckled her toes, forcing her to withstand the sight, the sensations before moving up. "And here…" He bit into her calves, kneading them with his teeth as he trailed up to her inner thigh. "And here…" Her body contorted under his onslaught.

Suddenly he hissed like a geyser about to blow, his hands digging in her buttocks. He'd seen the henna patterns there.

On an explosive expletive, he knocked her legs wide with his shoulders, lunged between them.

She squirmed, trembled, tried to squeeze her legs closed. "You, please, I want you, *you,* inside me, now please now…"

He looked up at her, eyes like twin infernos, sable hair cascaded over his leonine forehead. Then with his mouth set in cruel intent, he slid up her body, igniting every fuse along the way until he lodged his hardness at her entrance through his clothes, had her whimpering, "Yes, yes, please, yes."

In answer he only knocked her clamping legs from around his hips, came over her, straddled her midriff, loosened his pantaloons enough to show her his shaft.

A clench of intimidation sank its talons into her gut at his girth and length, at his beauty and sleekness. She craved his invasion, not only for the ecstasy it forced from her flesh, but because when he occupied her, she was intimate with his power and maleness, the potency of his desire, with his essence. With him. Giving her pleasure without union now wasn't a reward but a punishment.

He held his shaft, doing what her hands, imprisoned by his thighs, burned to do, stroking himself inches from her lips.

"Is this what you want most, Carmen?" Her nod was frantic, a tear slipping from one eye, trickling to her ear as she writhed beneath him, trying to free her hands, to get them on his flesh. "You told me you had your most intense orgasms with me inside you. Is that true, or were you catering to my ego?"

She renewed her efforts to escape the prison of his body, have him where she needed him, her heart stampeding with futility. "True…it's true, please, please…"

He tightened his waistband again, widened his thighs, let her pull her arms out only to clamp her hands, raised them for her to look at. "You think you can wear my name like this…" He dismounted her, twisted her toward the mirror to show her his hand slipping between the cheeks of her hennaed buttocks. "And this, and go unpunished, Carmen? For this you don't get what you crave most."

He pushed her onto her back, nudged her folds apart with deft fingers, before descending to replace them with his tongue.

He licked a taste, breathed her in, let his appreciation growl out over her engorged flesh, sending her screeching and scratching. He groaned his pleasured pain. "This is for every time you wrote my name on your delectable flesh. I'll torment you, like you tormented me every second of the past sixteen months."

Ignoring her protests, he took the lips of her core in a voracious kiss, tonguing her, thrusting light then hard, sweeping short then long, suckling, layering sensation until she was buried. He brought her to the edge, snatched her away, never pushing her over, too many times to count, no doubt the number of times his name marked her body.

When her breath fractured, her pleas stifled, and she lay beneath him paralyzed with hyperstimulation, he talked into her, sending the shock of each vibration, each syllable throughout her system. "Next time it's me who'll write my name all over you. But right here…" He pinpointed the bud where all her nerves converged, took it in a sharp nip. "I'll tattoo my name."

The discharge of all the pent-up stimulation was so explosive, she heaved in detonation after detonation until she felt her spine might snap.

He had no mercy, pushed three fingers inside her, sharpening her pleasure, lapping up its flood until her voice broke. He didn't stop even then, sucked every spasm and aftershock out of her, blasting her sensitized flesh with more growls. "And this is to get you ready for what you deserve for walking out on me." Two fingers sawed inside her spasming channel while one beckoned at her internal trigger, his thumb echoing the action on its mirror image outside. She writhed under the renewed surge, the need for release a rising crest of incoherence. She thrust against his hand until his rumbled *"Marrah Kaman"*—*one more time*—hurled her convulsing and shrieking into another orgasm.

He came up to loom over her, watching her trembling with what he'd done to her, watching his hand tracing the patterns of his name on her buttock. Mute, saturated with pleasure, hungrier for him than ever, she watched him, the emotions on his face coming too fast and thick for her to register, to decipher. To withstand.

Melting with the barrage, with needing him to end his punishment, give her the punishing ride she was dying for, she wrenched her eyes away, down. He was jutting against his pantaloons, the crown of his shaft straining beyond the waistband, wide and thick and daunting, dark and glistening with craving, throbbing with control. The moment he freed her hands to strip off her armbands, she lunged to snatch his pants down.

He caught her hands. "Even now you stand by your claims that you need me inside you for the most intense climax?"

She bucked her hips at him, begging. "I'm still conscious am I not? Still hungry, hungrier…" She was stunned to find her voice hoarse not gone. "I crave everything you do to me, your every touch turns me inside out with pleasure, but when you're inside me, it's…it's indescribable…"

Lava simmered in his gaze, the rest of him freezing. She made use of his stillness, skimmed stinging hands over the silk skin and hair-covered steel of his pecs, his abs, following the pattern with her lips and tongue while her hands delved beneath his waistband, closed on his engorgement.

He lay on his side, letting her worship him. He waited until she thought she'd fulfilled her hunger, was kissing the satin head, licking the precious flow of his arousal, let her get a full sample of his feel and taste and thickness as he thrust into the moist heat of her hunger, once, before he reared back, left her choking with chagrin and deprivation.

"This is my feast, Carmen. You are." He snatched a pile of pillows, arranged them, dropped her back on top of them, had her arched, prostrated for his domination with an urgency bordering on violence, kneeled between her spread thighs, took her buttocks in his hands, his fingers digging shards of pain and frenzy into her. "And this is just to take the edge off…"

"Just do it…tear into me, tear me apart…*please*…"

He did. He rammed into her. All his power and the accumulation of frustration and hunger behind the thrust. The head of his erection, nearly too wide for her, mashed against all the right places, abrading nerves into an agony of response, pushing receptors over the limit of stimuli they could take, the gush of sensation they could transmit. He'd forged halfway inside her when she screamed, arched up in a deep bow, going into a paroxysm as the world flickered out, diffused, only his beloved face in focus, clenched in pleasure, his eyes vehement with his greed for hers.

And what she'd heard was true. Sex *was* better after her operation, her great loss. Blindingly, excruciatingly better. Orgasm raged through her, discharging in blow after blow of pleasure so sharp it was agony.

She raved, begged. "Can't…can't…please…you…you…"

He understood. Gave her what she needed. The sight of his face seizing, the feel of him succumbing to the ecstasy she gave him, the hard jets of his climax inside her. They hit her at her peak, had her thrashing, weeping, unable to endure the spike in pleasure. Everything blipped, faded…

Heavy breathing and slow heartbeats echoed from the end of a long tunnel as the scent of sex and satisfaction flooded her lungs. Awareness trickled back into her body, which was a mess of tremors, so sated it was numb. She felt one thing, though. Farooq. Still inside her, even harder, larger. She opened lids weighing half a ton each, saw him swim in and out of focus, still kneeling between her legs, her hips on his thighs, one palm kneading her breasts, the other gliding over her shoulders, her arms, her belly.

"So it does take orgasming around me to knock you out."

"Told you so…" Her head flopped to the side, her heart following at the sight they made, the image of erotic abandon, half out of their wedding fineries, his ruined, their hair tousled, her face shell-shocked, his taut, savage, her position the image of wantonness, her arms thrown over her head, arched back over the pillows he'd piled beneath her, her hips jutting, her legs opened over his hips, his shaft half-buried inside her, stretching her glistening entrance, her lips wrapped around him in the most intimate kiss. And he was watching her watch them.

He gave her more to watch, thrust two more inches inside her.

"You were right…" she slurred at his deepening occupation, her tongue feeling anesthetized, swollen in her mouth. "This…is the edge of…survival. My heart…almost burst. I don't know if this—" a lethargic finger indicated her twisting tongue "—is from a stroke…or if the paralysis…will wear off. If this was just…to take the edge off the hunger…the main course might well be fatal."

He set his teeth as he rocked another inch inside her. "If ever there was a woman who can take a man to the limits of his mortality with her passion, it's you, Carmen. It's only fair I reciprocate in kind."

Her voluntary functions were shot to hell. Her thrust to accept more of him had to be some autopilot, set on Farooq. "We had…this conversation…before…"

"Your limited experience is irrelevant." He thrust deeper into her, the lubrication of their combined pleasure smoothing his advance. "You're a natural-born femme fatale."

Her hand moved under some external power, but with her hunger, trembled down the center groove of his abdomen to his shaft, to where they were merged. "Your femme fatale?"

"*B'haggej'Jaheem*—by hell, you are. *Mine*." He ground deeper into her, reaching the point where the familiar expansion inside her turned into almost-pain. An edge of dominance, a sharpness of sensation that was glorious, addictive, overwhelming, even a little frightening. The idea of all that he was, melding with her, at her mercy as she was at his, filled volumes inside her, body and mind and soul. "Say it, *ya* Carmen. *Enti melki.*"

"*Ana melkak*...I'm yours, yours...Farooq, darling, please..."

At the word *darling* he snarled something colloquial she didn't get, took the edges of her *lehenga*'s zipper in both hands...and ripped. She lurched in mortification.

He growled again. "I'll have a dozen made for you, must see you...all of you..."

Still lodged inside her, he freed her from her torn clothes, his hands and eyes everywhere he exposed. She closed her eyes at the starkness of his appreciation, at the ferocity of anticipation. Now, he'd really make love to her...

He moved. But he wasn't feeding her more of him. He was leaving her body. Her eyes tore open in panic, whimpering at his loss, her fingers too feeble to stop him. Cold shuddered through her. But it wasn't that of losing her clothes or his heat.

His gaze on her lower belly was the source of frost.

"You have a scar."

Eleven

Carmen bit a lip that trembled out of control.

She couldn't talk about it. About her imperfections and losses. But oh God, he looked so…grim. Did he feel them? Did the external evidence of them put him off, now the edge had dulled?

"You had a Cesarean." She nodded. His eyes turned almost all-black. "Did it hurt?"

She tried to laugh, managed a sound of distress rather than mockery. "I clung to the drug-free route only until they told me Mennah was obstructed and was in fetal distress. Then I was screaming for them to give me every drug they had and to open me up. From then on, I can assure you I felt no pain."

"You know I meant afterward."

She knew. And she didn't want to answer. Didn't want to remember the pain that had made her weep as she'd nursed Mennah, the debilitation that had turned caring for her daughter, moving at all, into torture. She couldn't tell him any of it. He'd suspect that more than a surgical wound had caused her agony. And he'd be right. Her endometriosis had flared up to crippling levels until she'd given in, did the only thing that would put her back on her feet to be a mother for Mennah—removing the source of trouble. She'd had a hysterectomy three weeks after Mennah's birth. The reopened scar had hurt then, had taken weeks to heal. And she'd been unable to take painkillers while she nursed her baby.

"It hurt," he said when she didn't answer, his voice vibrating with conviction, with a fury over it. "And you didn't have anyone to take care of you, or Mennah for you. You *fool*."

He suddenly heaved up to his feet, tore his clothes off his body like a madman, every sinew and muscle straining as if against a crushing weight, his engorged manhood erect flat against his steel abs. He still wanted her.

Those difficult tears she'd learned to shed since she'd known him burned at the back of her eyeballs, two breaking the barrier of her resistance, corroding a path to her chin.

He descended on her like a great vulture, pulling her to him, slamming her against his overheated flesh, demanding, "Why the tears, *ya ghalyah?*"

Oh God. His endearment. The one he'd always called her. Precious. Treasured. He'd made it hers again. The sentinel tears were followed by a flood. "I thought the scar put you off, that I—I'm…"

"A fool a thousand times over." He gave her one quick shake, ending her doubts. "I crave nothing but you."

His teeth pressed into her lower lip, with enough force to still it, to show her the power of his craving. He groaned long and deep as he applied more pressure until she whimpered, opened her mouth, her hands clenching around his neck, her breasts crushed to his chest, cushioning him, one leg clamping his hip, a carte blanche for anything he'd do to her.

When her undulations against him became quakes, he suckled her lips into his mouth, in long, smooth pulls, drawing more plumpness into her flesh, running his tongue inside them, drawing more of her taste until her whimpers became incessant. Only then did he plunge into her with tongue and ferocity. He drained her, then tore his lips from hers, trailed them over her cheeks, jaw, neck, breasts, nibbling and suckling her to madness. Then he reached her scar.

What he did then almost ruptured her heart.

He pressed his face against it, nudging her like an affectionate lion, groaning. "This is where you gave me Mennah, the source of her miracle, and of the pain you endured alone. This binds you to me, makes you *aghla*, more precious, makes me want you more, when I didn't know there could be more wanting."

She hiccupped an intake of distress. It hurt beyond measure, whether she feared he didn't want her or she knew he did. Everything he did or said affected her with an intensity that ended up simulating pain. But it was worse now.

His lips were on her scar, paying homage, and for terrible moments, she felt a phantom womb convulse inside her. Primal longings burst there, to have his manhood driving into her as it once had, so huge and powerful it had breached her cervix, what remained of the core of her femininity, splashed his seed directly where the overriding forces of her love and his potency had smashed the odds, done the impossible, created the miracle of Mennah.

There would be no more miracles. Her potential had been amputated, and she'd been left clinging to her miracle with a desperation that might have suffocated her child, if Farooq hadn't found them.

The emptiness inside her hadn't hurt, had lain dormant, forgotten. But the wound had gaped with his reappearance, the loss damaging only with the yearning to be a whole woman for him.

He, as always, was the source of her agony.

And only he could make it bearable.

She grabbed him, tears splashing over him as she threw herself into the abyss of unrequited love.

"I feel so empty without you, darling," she choked. "I missed you...the emptiness is too huge, fill it—fill me, Farooq, again please...."

"Sahrah." He threw his head back at her invocation, calling her a witch on an elemental groan, his face twisting in carnal suffering as something seemed to shatter inside him. He plunged into her with all the force of the snapping momentum.

She screamed at the piercing fullness, beyond her capacity...tearing her apart... "Yes, Farooq, *yes*..."

But he rested inside her, possessed her lips in another exercise of abandon. She opened for his tongue, each plunge tightening her around his invasion in a vise until he growled, *"Ya Ullah,* so tight, so *right*..."

Next second, he was withdrawing from her depths.

The implosion was crippling. *"Farooq."*

In answer to her desperation he hauled her around him, bit her ear on a rough "Hang on" that had her digging her heels into his buttocks. He stood on the bed, stepped down from it, strode with her wrapped around him to the dining table set in the perfection of their wedding night dinner, set her on its edge. Then he reached behind her and sent everything crashing to the floor.

His violence jolted through her with a jumble of reactions. Consternation at his disregard for the things he'd destroyed, elation at his impatience to resume their merging, and fright.

"The glass...your feet..." she gasped.

He plastered her back to the cool mahogany, had her legs splayed, a hungry embrace for his bulk, her feet braced at the edge. "The wreckage is nowhere near me. From where I'm standing, the only injury I'm risking is a heart attack at your beauty, *ya jameelati.* Tomorrow I'll make an altar of this height and serve you on top of it." He plunged inside her again, filling her beyond her limits with every power and weakness. She was master and slave. Goddess and worshipper. His hands roamed over her, following the twin suns of his eyes, exacting every intimacy as he thrust inside her in an escalating rhythm, watching her climb, arch, seek. The volcanic core of an orgasm built inside her again and he came over her, gave her his weight to writhe under, his mouth to mate with, his fingers sliding between them, stimulating the focus of need, unlocking the code only he knew.

He gulped down every screech of her new climax, making it double as he exploded inside her, feeding her convulsions to the last twitches, pouring the fuel of his pleasure on hers.

It might have been another day, another age when she came back into her body, still keening, her teeth deep in his flesh, her most profound thanks for the torment and the satisfaction.

He extricated her fangs from his shoulder, his smile feral as he withdrew from her body. Even lost in the bliss and stupor of postorgasm devastation, she still moaned at his loss, at the sight of his erection still in full glory, glistening with the mixture of their pleasure.

He yanked her up, slamming her into his chest. "Don't worry. I'm far from finished with you."

He raised her up until her limp body hung above him at arm's height, kept her there looking down on him, half-fainting with satiation, still shuddering with aftershocks. Then he let her slide down his sweat-slick landscape, caught her lips. Just as she caught fire again, sought him, he caught her hands.

"I said *I* wasn't finished with you." With hands filled with cherishing power, he turned her, laid her facedown on the table, her bottom jutting off its edge, her toes barely touching ground. She discovered another mirror flanking the dining area. He'd positioned it for the best view of the next stage in her enslavement. "Now I'll find out how many times you have my name written in that maze. Here's one." He bent, nipped the tip of her shoulder blade. "Two." His blunt nail scratched half an inch beside it. "Three..."

She lay there, helpless, watching him own her in their reflection, play her like a virtuoso, loving the game he'd invented, loving him as he reclaimed her every response and inch, sliding gossamer touches down her every sensitivity, sowing bites and suckles, knowing, pleasuring, punishing her every lightning-inducing switch until she felt her insides charring with the beauty, the expectation. The frustration.

So there was such a thing as torture by stimulation. Possibly death by arousal. He had unlocked her multiorgasmic potential, but surely those megaton orgasms should be all her nervous system could handle? How could she want more of him?

That's why it's called addiction, idiot. The more you have, the more desperately you want him.

When she felt she'd shudder apart she cried, "Just *take me.*"

"Take you, Carmen? You mean like this?" He slammed into her. She cried out at the abruptness of his invasion. He withdrew all the way out then slammed back, with even more power, forcing a sharper screech from her depths. "Or like this?"

"Farooq—yes!" She clawed at the smooth surface beneath her, putting all her strength behind thrusting back into his assault. She fought with him for deeper, harder, hating the inequality of their positions.

Then he lay on her back, his hands around her, under her, completing his exploitation, stroking her, stoking her inside and out into another blinding orgasm. On the final shearing spasms he joined her, exploding into a roar of completion, his seed filling her to overflowing.

She lay pressed between now-warm, moist wood and warmer, moister living steel, full, fulfilled, wishing to remain fused with him forever. But he was ending it.

She felt him receding from her. In every way.

"Farooq?"

Farooq gritted his teeth at the tremolo of her call. At its power. She'd again offered herself, made him forget his resolutions. To keep it about carnal pleasures and nothing more. He'd even demanded confessions from her. And she'd freely offered them. *Ya Ullah,* the things she'd said...

And he still had no proof he could trust her. Yet he had. He'd believed her every word, every gasp and scream and tear.

Then he'd seen her scar and he'd been swamped. By the depth of the blessing she'd bestowed on him, what she'd had to endure to do it. Everything in him raged that he hadn't been there to hold her *ala kfoof er-raha*—on the hands of comfort and cosseting, his princess in his cocoon of pampering and protection. He'd wanted to develop temporal powers to wrench back time, go to her in her hours of need, absorb her pain and fear. He'd wanted to swear that next time he'd be there from the first second, for every heartbeat afterward. He hadn't.

He'd said enough. *Ya Ullah,* the things *he'd* said...

And beyond words, the way he'd lost all sense of self in her, surrendered to her as she'd dragged him into their dimension of carnal excess and sensory overload, spilled himself three times inside her in the delirium of ecstasy, each time with the image of all this pleasure forming another miracle like Mennah. She could already be pregnant again. The wish that she was, or soon would be, the need to tether her to him by any means, spread through him like a mind-altering drug...

La ya moghaffal—no, you fool. Stop.

He must decide how to proceed, couldn't go back and take her again. Not on her terms. He had to set new ones before he did. As he would. As he had to. His sac felt heavy and painful again, his erection straining, every inch stinging to feel her beneath him, around him. And that was only the physical part. Everything else in him was clamoring for her. Her voice, her eyes, her wit, her hunger. Her warmth and sincerity...?

He struggled to deny the pangs as he ignored her tremulous call, crossed his space to the bathroom. He felt her gaze following him, her confusion and hurt palpable.

He gritted his teeth against their influence, entered the

bathroom, crossed to the huge sunken tub, hit the heat-regulating buttons, started it. He'd soak. Until this seizure of hunger passed. Until she went to bed…

"Is this what I should expect from now on?"

Don't turn. Send her to bed. Don't look at her.

He turned, looked at her. He'd known he shouldn't have.

She was naked, as he'd left her, the cascade of her hair a burst of color under the spotlights among her paleness. She looked like a mermaid who'd suddenly grown legs and was thrown on land, unsure how to stand. Her voluptuousness bore the marks of his eroded restraint, her thighs slick with the ecstasy he'd found inside her, her shoulders hunched, her arms hugging her middle as if bracing against crippling pain.

"We have sex, then you walk away?"

She called the chain reaction of cataclysms they'd just shared *sex?* But then, he'd treated it as such.

"You expected cuddling?" he bit off, furious, with her, with himself. "Expected the old Farooq?"

He could swear he felt something inside her quiver before it shattered. Hope? For what? The clean slate she'd asked for? Or a renewed hold on him for a new plot?

Her eyes reddened. But their expressiveness, which for their six magical weeks and throughout this night had told him she was his in every way, was expunged, as if she'd ceased to…exist.

"I just needed to know what to expect. Now I know. When you get tired of me, will you let me move out of your quarters?"

"Who says I'll get tired of you?"

"The old Farooq. He gave me three months, of which I served half. Should I expect that after serving the other half, whatever fascination I hold for you will be depleted and you'll let me go, let me be Mennah's mother only?" As he'd thought in her apartment. A few lifetimes ago. "Or have you decided you have a taste for hurting and humiliating me after all?"

"Enough," he snarled. "You've changed your tune again,

I see. All through the night you've begged for me, been mine and now…"

"Now it doesn't matter what I am. It never mattered. To you or to anyone else. It's what *you* are that matters. What you do, what you decide. I'm not in your league, Farooq. You pointed that out to me early on. As if I needed to be told. You'll do what you want, and I have no say in the matter." Without warning tears splashed her face, her arms, the ground. "I only ask, for Mennah's sake…don't destroy me."

It was the most macabre thing he'd ever seen. Her face, as vacant as a corpse's, flooded in tears streaming from eyes so red he felt they'd start gushing blood any second.

This was real. Wasn't it? He could trust her. Couldn't he? He couldn't bear it if he was hurting her and she didn't deserve it. If she was and had always been his. If she loved him…?

He wanted to say…everything. But he couldn't. He had to make sure first. Because once he said it…*he'd be hers, too.* Forever.

He must find out if she was his, the same way. His heart and mind said yes. Now he had to await the verdict of time.

But he couldn't abide time now, couldn't bear her tears one more second. Couldn't stand to see her turning away after she'd given him the most sublime night of his life. After she'd given him all of herself. And tonight, she had. This he *was* certain of.

"Carmen, come here." She didn't stop. He strode after her, caught her at the threshold of his expansive bathroom, took hold of shoulders that slumped with defeat. "Come, Carmen."

Her tears flowed undeterred as she said, "Again? I'm sorry *somow'wak,* but this is probably beyond my physical abilities right now. I know you're used to making things happen with a word, and in my case, with a touch, but after sixteen months, and even though I begged you for every bit of it as you pointed out, having you three times will probably leave me unable to walk for a week."

And he laughed. Was there no end to her surprises?

Next second his laughter died. The burst of insight was blinding. She was trying to blind him to her tears, her weakness, using quips. Her wit was her only weapon against him.

Suddenly he hated that the power imbalance between them was so immense. He could balance it with three words. But those might unbalance it in his enemies' favor. And he wasn't just a man with his own heart, faith and life on the line. He would soon have Judar's, the whole *region's* fate resting on his clarity and decisiveness.

For now, he would obey, his instincts, not the murkiness of the doubts that had poisoned him for so long.

He cupped her face in his palms, damned himself when her teeth chattered as her features crumpled, her eyes those of a woman who would welcome the assurance of despair over the cruelty of hope.

"Your eyes are the first things that caught me, Carmen. Rivaling Judar's skies and seas in their openness, their depths. They make me see how the Arabian Nights tale in which the tears of a princess drowned a kingdom wasn't so ludicrous. Yours could drown a realm. I would kiss them away, stem the tears as I've been their source, but we have a saying here. *El boassah fel ain tefar'raa.*"

That stopped her tears. "A kiss in the eye separates?" He nodded. She hiccupped. "And you consider that a bad thing?"

"I can't think of a worse thing."

Her expression became lost. "Hot or cold, Farooq. Choose one temperature and stick with it. Please."

"I can't, when neither serves or applies. Scorching and incendiary still don't, *ya ajmal makhloogah.*" She moaned at his endearment, the most beautiful creature, squeezed eyes that leaked again. He bent, swung her up in his arms. "About not being able to walk for a week, who said you have to? Your feet won't touch the ground, *ya Ameerati.*" He took her to the sunken bath, descended into the perfect-temperature water.

Their groans of aching relief at its fluid embrace echoed each other. "As for your physical limitations, let's see how far we can stretch them…"

And he stretched them far, proved to her he could make her come again as he soothed the soreness he'd inflicted on her, stroking and suckling her to a dozen gentle orgasms before he let her melt back against him, drained but somehow awake in the warmth of water and intimacy. Then he took her back to their marriage bed, cuddled her as his heart dictated, not like the old Farooq would have, but as the new one who felt far more, far, far deeper.

As she slipped into sleep, he clung to her swollen lips one last time, told her all he could tell her at the moment.

"I will never get enough of you, Carmen."

"It's such a pleasure to see you and *Maolai* Farooq, so happy, *ya Maolati.*"

Carmen couldn't look at Ameenah. Mennah was standing, seemed determined to take her first step today. Maybe even right now.

Oh God, she had to call Farooq. "Ameenah, my cell, please, the one with the hotline to Farooq. And my video cam."

Ameenah zoomed out of the room. Carmen barely breathed, not daring to show any reaction to throw Mennah's concentration off. Ameenah was back in seconds.

Just as Carmen turned on her cam, was about to hit the dial button to summon Farooq with shrieks of urgency to see this milestone with her, Mennah sat down, crawled away and busied herself with the cubes Farooq had gotten her yesterday. He had then spent the entire evening playing with Mennah and Carmen.

Smiling in self-deprecation, at her still-booming heart, at the false alarm she'd been about to raise, she thanked God Mennah had pulled the plug on this situation when she had. Farooq had a vital state meeting, but at her word he would have dropped everything and come hurtling over here only to find a sitting daughter and a terminally embarrassed wife waiting for him.

Carmen looked at the broadly smiling Ameenah and sighed. "You were saying something when I sent you on that wild-goose chase?"

Ameenah repeated her previous statement, and Carmen only smiled. She was wrong. They weren't happy. They were delirious. At least, she was. He was…better than her old incomparable Farooq.

After their history-making wedding night, he'd seemed to let go, the bouts of anger and suspicion fading, his ups and downs becoming ups that kept only heightening. Their nights were intensifying infernos of ecstasy and abandon, and he no longer pulled away afterward, coming closer instead, letting down his guard until she felt he'd let her in all the way. Their days, which he designed with utmost care for leisurely family time with her and Mennah, followed a pattern of escalating joy.

It had been six weeks now, completing the time she'd thought she'd have before he had enough of her. But true to his word, he hadn't. He seemed to want more of her, and then more. In and out of bed.

They made heart-melting love and had recuperation-needed-afterward sex. They shared times that flowed from serious and contemplative to tender and bantering to teasing and hilarious. He started depending on her experience and counsel, delegated responsibilities to her, for the first time entrusting vital details to another. And in every possible situation, he was letting her skills and imagination soar to their full potential.

No, this wasn't happiness. This was bliss.

So much bliss that her heart hit the ground at random moments, with fear so brutal, she couldn't breathe.

When would it come to an end?

Then Ameenah added, "I only hope you won't let your happiness be affected when it's time for *Maolai* to do his duty."

And she knew. *Now* was when. She rasped, "What duty?"

Ameenah's eyes rounded with horror as she realized she'd slipped up, no doubt seeing her statement's impact on Carmen. "*Ya Elahi, ana assfah—Maolati samheeni,* I beg your forgiveness, I didn't mean to…"

Her heart started to implode. "Stop apologizing and freaking out, Ameenah. Now tell me what this duty is."

"If *Maolai* hasn't told you, it isn't my place—"

Carmen raised a hand. "It is your duty to do as I say, isn't it? Now I'm telling you to tell me."

After an oppressive minute, Ameenah said, "*Maolai* is to enter a marriage of state."

The world disappeared, the void outside joining the void inside, until she felt she would be no more…

"When?" Was that disembodied voice hers?

Ameenah was on the verge of tears by now. Carmen felt nothing as Ameenah choked, "No one knows. The bride hasn't even been picked yet."

"Why not?"

"It's a complicated story, and I'm not the one best equipped to tell it to you…"

Carmen interrupted her agitation. "You're my best friend around here, and if you won't tell me, I'll only be in the dark, and miserable. *Please*…tell me."

Ameenah finally nodded. "It started six hundred years ago…"

A bleeding huff burst out of Carmen. "God, it was preordained Farooq would marry someone else that far back?"

"It was that far back that the Aal Masoods ended the tribal wars and founded Judar. But ever since King Zaher fell ill, Judar's second-most influential tribe, the Aal Shalaans, started demanding their turn at the throne, threatening an uprising. Offering them settlements didn't work, and a forceful solution seemed the one remaining option. A solution that would lead to civil war. A war the Aal Masoods will do anything to prevent. Even if it means giving up the throne. Which would still tear Judar apart."

Carmen stared at her. Wow. Farooq couldn't be involved in anything that wasn't world-shaking, world-*shaping,* could he? Was it any wonder he'd shaken hers, shaped it?

Ameenah went on. "Then our neighboring kingdom, Zohayd, was dragged into the crisis. The Aal Shalaans form the ruling house and the majority of the population there, and they started pressuring King Atef to support their tribesmen's rise to Judar's throne. He refused. The Aal Masoods are his biggest allies and the reason behind Zohayd's and the region's prosperity, and their losing the throne would destabilize the whole region, maybe the world. His refusal was about to plunge Zohayd in civil war, too.

"But through the Aal Masood brothers' intensive negotiations, the Aal Shalaans accepted a peaceful solution. That the future king of Judar would marry the daughter of their noblest patriarch so their blood would enter the royal house of Aal Masood. The problem is, after much deliberation, that patriarch was determined to be the king of Zohayd himself, who has no daughter."

This kept getting better and better. Carmen felt twinges of hysteria rising through the numbness. "So now what?"

"They're in negotiations again," Ameenah rasped, as if confessing a crime. "Over picking another patriarch, I guess."

"And once this happens, Farooq will marry his daughter, to stop the whole region from going to hell in a handcart."

"Yes. But, *Maolati,* this won't affect you, you mustn't let it. You are the wife he picked himself, the one he loves."

She burst out laughing, shocking Ameenah like she'd once shocked her husband. This *was* a prime example of *sharr el-baleyhah ma yodhek*—the worst plights induce laughter.

She'd been tormenting herself with all the reasons it would end, and now she was going to lose him over something she couldn't have imagined. She couldn't even be angry that he'd married her knowing he'd take another wife. Farooq sure married only for momentous reasons. His daughter's future, now Judar's—the whole region's.

He'd marry another woman, come to *her* after copulating with that woman to produce the heir who'd avert civil wars…

She gestured for Ameenah to leave her, dropped her head to her knees, doubling over from the disemboweling pain. Jealousy. The one thing she hadn't suffered on his account. He'd been with her alone before. He had this integrity. But now, if all she felt for him was compounded by marrow-eating jealousy, her sanity *would* fray…

No. The moment he took another wife, she'd retreat from his life, become Mennah's mother only again. This meant one thing.

She had to take every breath she could of him, while she could, to hoard the memories for the nothingness ahead.

She pressed the dial button. Farooq answered before the second ring. "Carmen." His voice shook her with the intimacy he made of her name, the magic, with the roughness that carried his perpetual hunger. "What does *Ameerati el ghalyah* want?"

Desperation rose with the mercilessness of a sandstorm.

"I want *you*, Farooq. *Now*."

Twelve

Farooq tore through the palace, had people dashing out of his way as they would out of the path of an out-of-control vehicle.

They were wise to recognize the danger in the eagerness that rattled his bones. Just as his opponents had. None had dared make their annoyance known when he'd walked out on the negotiations the moment Carmen had demanded him. Another first that only Carmen could induce. His Carmen. His.

Certainty had been blossoming during the last glorious six weeks. Endless details, momentous and trivial, all incontestable, had reinforced the verdict of his heart. She *was* his. Had always been. Tareq had lied. She'd never been his mole. The only solid evidence of that had been the words of a man who lived to lie. The rest was circumstantial, with a dozen explanations now that he believed his Carmen would never do anything that wasn't rooted in nobility and self-sacrifice. He had his proof in everything she was. He'd never bring it up, would never insult her with the inventions of the opportunistic pervert who'd claim-jumped her desertion, twisted it as he did everything to serve his purposes.

But Tareq no longer mattered. Nothing else did. Only Carmen.

Still…there was something about her that troubled him. Not him as Prince Aal Masood, but as her husband and lover. Something, an elusiveness, even through all her surrender and magnanimity, that stopped him from balancing the power between them once and forever. His mind had left the gravity of negotiations to ponder what else he could possibly need from her. Then she'd called, and he'd realized. This was what he'd been waiting for. For her to initiate intimacy, letting down the last barrier, trusting him unconditionally as he'd come to trust her. Did she also know that by doing so, she was invoking her ownership of him?

He stopped in front of their door, racked with emotions. He was ready to be claimed, body and soul, to relinquish all power to her. His voice, his fingers shook as he operated the door, posed on the threshold of the rest of his life.

He stepped inside and she sprang yet another surprise on him.

She charged him, climbed him, wrapped herself around him. He stood for a long moment, claimed, surrounded, deluged in her hunger, drowning in her ferocity. Then he staggered to their bed, his arms filled with happiness made flesh, made woman. His woman. He tried to lower her to the bed, but she twisted in his arms, made him change direction, take her on top.

He saw her then, rising above him, the flames of her hair scorching down on him, her body enveloped in another of those mind-messing creations that echoed her coloring, something semi see-through, stretched over her every perfection, showcasing her, hiding enough to send his imagination tearing through it. Which he would probably end up doing. He touched her and forgot how clothes where supposed to be taken off. But it was her face, her eyes, what he saw and felt there that sent his arousal shooting from distressing to life-threatening, catapulted his spirit on its first rocketing flight.

This. This was what he'd been born for. This woman. This being. This totality. *This.*

He took her lips, her tongue, letting her in, all the way, needing, living, *being,* in her, in their merging.

"All of you…I want all of you, Farooq…*all…*"

He drowned in the depths of her desire as she exposed him to its full measure, ignited fever all over him with touches and bites and suckles all the way down to the manhood he now knew had been created to mesh them together, to give her pleasure.

Then she devoured him. He let her, surrendered, spread himself for her to dominate, to pleasure, to drain.

His fingers shook in her hair, his body and heart in her power. After a life of sufficiency and restraint, of superiority, to feel such dependence was scary, transporting. Vital. He thrust his hips to her ravenous rhythm, sinking deeper into her hunger.

She drove her fingers into his buttocks, warning him not to draw away at his peak. "Give it all to me, darling…must have my fill…"

He had learned to give her this. He never had with others, just as he'd never foregone protection, both lines of intimacy he never wanted to cross. Until her, from the first night. In the past six weeks, she'd showed him beyond doubt there were no lines between them.

His hand convulsed in her hair as his loins exploded. She took his pleasure, lapped it up, climaxing, too, just from causing it, taking it, from rubbing against him to the rhythm of his release.

He snatched her up to his heart, communing in profound mouth-mating, sharing their descent. She reached for him again, knew she'd find him harder, crazed for more. She now knew that he achieved the heights of pleasure only inside her heat and giving, only in her pleasure.

She scampered over him, pushing him to his back, strad-

ling him, looked at him through tears that bound him, turning
er eyes to the seas he'd been lost in, never wanting to be
ound.

She held his erection against her scar, caressed him until he
as thrusting against her in torment. She rose to scale his length,
embled so much she failed, cried out, "I *want* you, Farooq."

"Carmen, *ya ghalyah*...yes, want me..." He helped her,
aised her, positioned himself at her entrance. "Feast on me,
now me how much pleasure I give you..."

She took him in one downward stroke. A whiteout of sen-
ation blinded him as her scorching honey engulfed him, his
ome inside her, his only home. His senses reignited when he
elt himself deep within her.

"Farooq..."

He understood her frenzy, rose with her impaled on him,
eaned against the mirror, held her buttocks in his palms.
Ride me, *ya rohi*. Take me and take your pleasure of me."

Her palms braced against the mirror, thighs trembling as
he tried to rise his length. She'd managed to slide up only half
f him when he engulfed one nipple while twisting the other.

Her palms slid off the mirror and she crashed on him, lodg-
ng him against her cervix, and wailed, *"Farooq...please..."*

"Lean on me, *ya habibati*." He placed her hands on his shoul-
ers then held her hips and moved her up and down his length
a leisurely journeys to the rhythm of his suckles and nibbles.

Then he told her. "Do you know how perfect you are? Do
ou feel what you're doing to me? I never dreamed pleasure
ke this existed. I never want to stop, stop pleasuring you,
iving to you."

"I can't...Farooq...can't...it's too much..."

Again he understood, put his power behind her back as he
olled to ease her onto it in the middle of the mattress, spread-
ng her knees wide-open with his bulk as he lunged forward,
iding up her flaming flesh. He undulated his hips, stretch-
ng her around his invasion yet again and stilled, throbbing in

her depths, rising above her. "Heaven would be nothing to being inside you." He withdrew as he spoke. Then holding her streaming eyes, he growled, "Take me, Carmen, take all of me." And he rammed back into her.

She screamed, her inner muscles squeezing his length in a fit of release. He rode the breakers of her orgasm in a fury of rhythm, feeding her frenzy. It went on and on until he felt her heart stampeding beneath his palm, saw her tears thickening feared he might be doing her damage.

"Come with me…"

Her sob as her seizure continued around him broke his dam. He let go, buried himself to her womb, wished he could bury all of himself inside her, and surrendered to the most violent orgasm he'd ever known, jetting his essence into her milking depths in gush after exhilarating gush, roaring his love, his worship.

"Ahebbek, aashagek, ya Carmen. Enti koll shai eli."

Carmen's consciousness didn't waver this time. The words exploding from Farooq's lips had blown it wide-open Blown her away.

I love you, I worship you. You're everything to me.

She lay inert beneath his beloved weight, filled with him with his roar, his words, their enormity mushrooming…

She felt him tear himself from her depths, pounce on her *"Ya Ullah, Carmen…breathe."*

But she'd forgotten how. He shook her and air rushed in almost bursting her lungs. She heard his choking relief, felt his kisses scorch off her skin, heard herself croak, "You said…said…"

"*Ahebbek? Aashagek? Amoot feeki?* And I *would* die for you."

"Stop, Farooq, stop…it's too much, too much…"

"*You* are too much. Everything you are, everything you make me feel. There's no one like you. You own me. *Ent habibati el waheeda, hob hayati. Enti hayati. Ana melkek.*"

You're my only love, the love of my life. You are my life. I 'n yours. Too much. "But how…when…?"

"How can I not love you and only you? You are not tailor-ade for me, you are created for me by God. As for when, 'om the first moment, and I fall in love with you again in very moment."

"But I never dreamed…"

"*I* never dreamed a woman like you existed. But you do, nd you're mine as I'm yours."

You can't *be mine. If you are, how can I ever give you up?*

"Carmen, *ma beeki?*" The emotions turning his magnifi-ent face incandescent dimmed. "You're not happy that I…?"

He stopped, as if he felt her anguish, and it hurt him.

She'd never let anything hurt him.

She surged into him, buried him under a storm of kisses nd tears. "I'm *not* happy, *somow'wak*. Happiness is an motion mere mortals induce, but you…you devastate me, ansfigure me, overwhelm me. No. None of that does you ustice. I'll have to invent new words to describe you, your ffect, what you make me feel."

He surged up, his face a display of all she'd attributed to im. "And you dare wonder how I love you? It took all I had, ying not to love you. All my struggles made me love you nore, *ya maboodati.*"

She collapsed over him, weeping again. He now thought nem tears of jubilation. As they were. Jubilation with an xpiration date. "Oh, darling…what I feel for you…that ou feel the same way…then you call me your soul and our life, and now your goddess…you're messing with my fe expectancy…"

"I'd give you mine. I'd give you all of it, *ya habibati.*"

She crashed her lips to his, silencing him. Every word, very expression on his adored face was impaling the spears nto her deeper. She panted for mercy. *"Habibi, er-ruhmuh…"*

He crushed her to him, kissed her back as ferociously, in-

undating her with his euphoria until emotional passion caugh
fire and they were fighting for a faster descent into delirium

It was dawn when the impetus of their hunger was satis
fied. She lay cocooned in his strength, his cherishing arms
His love. It was still, would always remain too huge to encom
pass, that she inspired the same emotions, the same devotion
in him.

But she didn't have always with him. She'd known tha
from the start. At first, because he was out of reach. Now, he
was within reach, but would soon drift out of it again. But, like
before, she'd think of the price later. She had now with him.

He rose above her, swept her with caresses, his love flaying
her with its beauty, its power. "*Hayati,* whenever you fee
ready, I want you to stop birth control. I can't wait to give
Mennah a brother. Or a sister. Hopefully both."

She smiled at him, went through the motions until he
wrapped himself around her, his hands caressing the abdomen
he was certain would soon swell with his child again.

She waited until his breathing evened in sleep, then let his
dreams detonate inside her, pulverize the now she had with
him to ashes.

It had been three weeks since Farooq had confessed his
love, asked her to stop birth control. She still hadn't confessed that she *really* didn't need it this time.

She couldn't cut her time with him short. She'd remain
with him until he left her to take a wife who would give him
more children. Give Mennah siblings…

Her phone rang. Thinking it must be a wrong number, she
snapped it up to reject the call. No one but Farooq called her
on this number, and he was in the shower.

Something made her press the answer button.

"*Ameerah* Carmen?"

Carmen's stomach lurched with instant dread and revulsion.
She remembered that androgynous voice. Tareq.

He went on, not waiting for an answer. "I'll get to the point. I want to meet with you."

She found her voice. "No."

"Don't be so quick to refuse. I'm doing you a favor."

"Thank you, but again, no. Goodbye, Prince Tareq."

He gave up the polite act, flayed her with malignancy. "You and your bastard daughter were the only thing standing between me and the throne. But not anymore. Your days as princess are numbered. I would still have offered you a generous settlement if you left now so that I could claim the succession sooner, but now I'll wait until my cousin throws you away as the useless tramp that you are. Yes, I investigated you, found out your…medical history. So it's goodbye to you, *ya somow'el Ameerah*. And good riddance."

She hurled the phone away as if it was a scorpion, and ran. Ameenah. She had to find Ameenah.

"Carmen…" Farooq called out after her as he came out of the bathroom. But she'd already closed the door.

His blood stirred again at the idea of catching up with her. But he had to put something on before he pursued her.

Huffing in frustration, he noticed her brick-red phone, their "hotline" phone, on the bed. She never went anywhere without it…

Something unfurled in his gut as he picked it up, accessed the call log. All his number. All but one.

He pressed the dial button. On the first ring a man answered. "I knew you'd change your mind."

He terminated the call. Tareq.

She'd been talking to Tareq.

And he'd said, *Change your mind.* About what?

What did it mean?

He exploded to his dressing room. He must find her, talk to her. He wasn't letting Tareq, or doubts, come between them again.

* * *

"What's Tareq's story?" Carmen closed the door behind her and Ameenah, still struggling with the agitation of her brush with Tareq. "Why was he bypassed for Farooq?"

Ameenah looked up at her out-of-the-blue question. "Tareq was never named crown prince, even though, with the deaths of both of King Zaher's younger brothers, he was first in line. When King Zaher said he would bypass Tareq for *Maolai* Farooq, Prince Tareq called in all the favors his greatly loved late father had with the most influential members of the Tribune of Elders, to pressure the king into changing his choice. So, King Zaher resorted to a measure no one would contest—making *Maolai* Farooq his crown prince in effect, but saying he would give the title to his own male child, when he had one. However, our queen is too old to be that child's mother, so to have an heir, the king would have to take another wife."

Carmen frowned. "Why was that a problem? Polygamy is sanctioned in Judar."

Ameenah made a gesture unique to the region, one signifying *yes—but*. "It has strict rules and requires the consent of the first wife. A consent she gave. But the Aal Masood's, especially their kings, are monogamous, and King Zaher couldn't do that to his queen, even to stop Tareq's rise to the succession."

"Tareq has a lot against him, huh?"

"Among many of his excesses, he is said to…favor, uh, boys…"

Whoa. A pedophile. "Then I'm surprised there was ever any problem in bypassing him. I'm surprised he wasn't stoned."

"He would have been, if his guilt was proved in a court of law. But his connections in the Tribune of Elders prevented that. He then declared he'd be the first king of Judar who never married, couldn't care less who the throne went to after him. That won him the Aal Shalaan's unwavering support and protection. It was then that King Zaher came up with what would assure *Maolai* Farooq of securing the succession, a requirement no one could contest—having a wife and a child as proof of stability and commitment to family."

Her breath caught. "When was that?"

"Just over eighteen months ago now."

Just around the time she'd walked out on Farooq.

Realizations piled up inside her head.

The king wouldn't have made this decree if he hadn't been confident Farooq would be married at once. Farooq could have had a suitable wife lined up…but no. He wouldn't have been wasting time with her when he should have been securing a marriage to protect the throne from Tareq. That meant one thing.

He'd been about to offer her marriage.

Maybe even the same night she'd left. And unknown to both of them, her pregnancy would have clinched the succession at once. But she'd walked out. And Tareq had helped her disappear.

It all made sense. "What happened then?"

"Prince Tareq married at once, into the only family of the Aal Shalaans who would take him. But his wife didn't conceive, and it was rumored he was undergoing fertility treatments. Then she did get pregnant, twice, but miscarried and was diagnosed with a condition that would make it impossible for her to carry a child to term. Tareq divorced her, and he's now married another."

"But why? The succession is already Farooq's."

Ameenah winced. "He'd gotten the Tribune to amend the king's ruling. Now a male child is needed to settle the succession."

So that was why Farooq wanted—no, *needed* a male child, at once. And he must be secure thinking she was probably pregnant by now, had no reason to suspect she was damaged, barren…Oh *God*.

She couldn't tell him, couldn't bear to. But she had to do what she'd known needed to be done. Retreat from his life.

Before it was too late…

* * *

Carmen had gone out, had taken her car and banned her guards from joining her. He'd waited for her to come back, refusing to jump to conclusions again.

She came into their quarters, pale, subdued. He went to her, tried to take her in his arms. His heart squeezed when she avoided them, dread rising as she stumbled to the far side of the room, overlooking the sea.

Then she said, "I want a divorce, Farooq."

And there was nothing left. In existence. In him.

She wasn't finished. "I—I beg you not to let this affect Mennah, that you'll let her have her mother."

He discovered many things were left. There was agony and disillusion and despair. There was a woman who'd conquered him, who'd taught him the meanings of unity and destiny and bliss, only to gut him and throw him into hell.

"What is Tareq paying you? *How* is he making you do this to me?"

She jerked at his accusation, her shoulders shaking. Was she crying? Shocked?

She *must* be. Now she'd turn, explain this insanity away…

She turned. "It doesn't matter, Farooq. Just let me go."

No. No. He'd only accused her to hear her denial, would have believed anything she said. But what she'd said implied her guilt.

He advanced on her, sanity draining in every step. "If you can side with a criminal like Tareq when I made you my princess, gave you my love, *myself,* I can't trust you near Mennah."

Horror shredded her numb mask. "*No.* You know I'm a good mother…please…I'll do anything if you let me stay near her…"

He hit bottom, knew he'd do anything to hang on to her. Even use Mennah. "You want Mennah, you remain my wife."

"But I'll never give you more children," she shrieked.

"Why?" he thundered. "Because you won't sleep with me now that your mission is accomplished? Now that you broke me?

It was she who broke down, heaped to the floor. Her anguish pummeled them both. The moment he could move, breathe, her broken whisper paralyzed him again.

"I had endometriosis. Was declared infertile by a dozen specialists...Steve divorced me because I couldn't provide an heir to his family fortune. That was why I thought it safe to make love without protection...why I ran from you to protect my miracle baby. After I had her my condition became crippling and I couldn't afford the endless procedures and the incapacitation when I had to take care of her. This scar is not only from my C-section. It is where I had a hysterectomy."

He staggered, the bolt of horror almost felling him. He clutched his head. *"Ya Ullah, ya Ullah..."*

Horror became panic as Carmen withered before his eyes. She'd misunderstood, was staggering up, stumbling away.

He caught her, tears he'd only ever shed on his father's and mother's graves scouring his face.

"Stop wasting time on me, Farooq," she wailed. "You might have jeopardized everything because of me already. But I didn't know, or I would have told you, risked anything, even seeing this look—oh God—*tears* in your eyes..."

"You think it's sadness for myself? It's all for you, for what you went through without me by your side, what you lost, what you might not have lost if I was there, giving you all the time and support to explore treatment options. I *am* agonized, for your agony and absolutely unfounded insecurities. You are more than I dreamed to have. I would have chosen you even if you hadn't given me Mennah. I *do* choose you, over the world."

"You *can't*," she screamed. "I thought I'd have more time with you, until you married the Aal Shalaan bride, but now you must marry any woman who can give you a male child before Tareq."

"You know everything...*ya Ullah...*" he choked.

Her nod was a quake. "That's why I didn't defend myself, so you'd leave me at once, while there was time to beat him to it."

"You'd do that for me? Paint yourself black…"

"I will do *anything* for you. You are my life. But I beg you, don't force me to stay near you, to see you in another woman's arms, see her get big with your child…"

She collapsed by degrees, clinging to him, ending up at his feet, racking sobs tearing her apart.

He stood paralyzed, a vise clamping his chest and back. This had to be how men lost their minds, had strokes and heart attacks. Being accosted by pain too big to encompass, loss too huge to endure. But no, he'd never lose her. Never.

"*Carmen, ahleflek ya maboodati,* I swear to you…"

What would he swear? That he didn't need a male child? That all she'd said wasn't true? It was. But it didn't have to be.

He swooped down, swept her up in his arms.

It was time to change a few truths.

"Carmen and I will not have more children, *ya Maolai.*"

Farooq had been about to demand an immediate audience with his uncle when the king beat him to it. He'd taken Carmen with him. Now she stood squirming in his hold, looking everywhere but at their king, who had eyes only for her, the new daughter he'd gained.

"I refuse the demand of providing a male heir for the succession. You must, too, or you'll be succumbing to Tareq's manipulation and to outdated notions. You yourself have no sons, and you are the happiest man I know with your wife and the daughters she gave you. You only worry about the succession because Tareq would make a disastrous king. I don't have that to worry about. I have my brothers as my successors, and I'm sure their children, when they one day have them, will be worthy successors, too."

Still casting his tired yet affectionate and compassionate

gaze on Carmen's bent head, the king said, "That's why I summoned you. I gathered the Tribune to debate the male child criterion. I reminded them a wife and child were proof of stability and responsibility, that the gender of the child is irrelevant and that we all know who between you and Tareq is king material. Things were up in the air until your latest intelligence on Tareq checked out as we convened. I presented the damning evidence but couldn't secure consent to a trial. I settled for banishing him from Judar and stripping him of his titles and wealth."

Still not daring to breathe, Carmen looked up at Farooq, who was clutching her as if he were afraid she'd dematerialize.

This meant…she had more time with him.

The king went on. "Now the succession is forever settled, you, my son, have to do your duty. I'm more sorry than I could express to ask you to do something I never could. But it's time for you to enter the marriage of state the peace treaty with the Aal Shalaans demands. I hoped we'd find another way, but it turns out King Atef has a daughter he never knew about from an American lover."

His gaze on Carmen grew more pained. "I know how painful this is, my daughter, but these are dangerous times, and if you love Farooq and have come to care for Judar, you'll consent to his second marriage."

"I—consent…" she rasped, tried to jerk free. Farooq's grip tightened. And she cried. "Just let me go, Farooq. Everything will be okay when I'm out of the equation."

Farooq clutched her harder. "I will *never* let you go, not in this life, and if I have any say, not in the next." She shook her head, splashing their arms with tears. "I never gave you a *mahr, ya rohi.* I couldn't decide on anything to do you justice. I just did." He turned to his uncle. "*Maolai,* I'm abdicating the succession to Shehab."

Farooq felt Carmen go rigid. His king's reaction was as dramatic. He looked…relieved. And Farooq understood why.

Even though he wanted Farooq to succeed him, he wanted him to be happy more. Wanted Carmen to be happy.

His answer seemed readymade. "I see this is your final decision, so I can only accept it. Just thank *Ullah* you have spare heirs as worthy as you of being king."

Carmen jerked out of his hold, in tears. "Are you both crazy? You're in the middle of a crisis that can change history and *you* say, I'm abdicating, and *you* just say, okay? No offense to Shehab, but how can anyone be as worthy as Farooq? I won't be the reason to deprive a nation of its most magnificent king…" She bit her lip. "No offense, King Zaher." She turned back to Farooq, the one to clutch him now. "You must fulfill your duty, remain crown prince, give Judar the marriage it needs. I take it back, Farooq, I take it back. I'll remain yours no matter what happens."

So there was more. More love. More wonder. Always would be with her. He hugged her off the ground. "*Ya rohi,* Judar's only loss today is losing you as its future queen. When I said I'm yours, I wasn't plying you with exaggerations. I was stating a fact. As unchangeable as my genetic code."

Her color neared that of her hair. "If you think you're proving anything to me, don't. This is bigger than us. I won't let you do something you'll regret—"

He silenced her with a kiss before he looked up, found his king watching them, moved but satisfied. He flashed him a smile. "*An eznak,* excuse me, *ya Maolai,* while I take this out of here. I believe this will end in a situation unsuited for your court."

Then he swept her away to their quarters as she protested and sobbed. He sat on their bed, dragged her on top of him, straddling his hips, and quieted her writhing into dwindling resistance.

"How about we make love first then argue later?" he purred.

"No. You must take it back before the king makes it public."

"Why must I, *ya hayati?* This is perfect. I rescued the succession from Tareq's claws. Now Shehab, who has never had a serious relationship and who won't mind marrying King Atef's daughter, will take it and her off my hands. I will become *his* crown prince, if one day he becomes king. I will remain second in line, as I lived most of my life. I've done my part for the throne, *ya roh galbi.* As for Judar, with you at my side—the best princess Judar will ever see—we'll accomplish great things."

"But you are the greatest man in the world, *ya habibi.* You'd be the best king. I think Shehab is great, too, but you, you…"

"I want only to be king of your heart."

Her weeping spiked. "Oh God…twenty-five years without shedding a tear, then I meet you and a lifetime accumulation floods out whether I'm happy or devastated. Now I'm both." She collapsed against his heart. "How is it possible that you love me as I love you? What have I ever done to deserve so much? How can I deserve it?"

"Just by being yourself, *ya rohi.* The most giving woman and mother, the most stimulating companion and the most addictive lover. No man, royal or otherwise, has ever dreamed of so much." He spread her on the bed. "About the addictive lover part…I need another fix…"

Hours later, he was lapping water over his armful of savagely pleasured and satisfied woman, murmuring his own pleasure into her clinging lips, over and over.

He'd finally convinced her that his abdication hadn't been an option but a necessity. Becoming king had been a duty, something he could relinquish. Being hers was his destiny.

"So what do you think of your *mahr?*"

She sighed her breath and taste into his mouth, the essence of love and satisfaction. "You had to go overboard, didn't you? Everything has to be world-shaking with you, doesn't it? I ask for one tiny clean slate, and you give up a throne for me."

He chuckled. Only his Carmen could talk like this, only her

words could make him feel like that. Invincible. Unparalleled. Blessed. "I take it you are impressed with my efforts?"

She traced patterns over his heart with fingers and lips. "If I was more impressed, you'd have to jump-start my heart."

"I trust you'll show proper awe and gratitude for the next sixty years or so?"

"You can certainly trust, *ya habibi.*" He knew nothing more certainly. That he could trust. Her. With his life. With everything. "And you know how inventive I can be."

"Indeed. I'm breathless to see, to experience, to thank the fates for your next brainstorm. Start inventing."

She twisted in the slickness of water and bubbles, gliding over his flesh, inventing new erogenous zones for starters, then proceeded to invent new reasons to love, new reasons to live.

As he knew she always would.

* * * * *

You've just finished Olivia Gates's powerful,
provocative debut book for Silhouette Desire.
But what will Shehab do to secure his kingdom?
Find out in THE DESERT LORD'S BRIDE,
second in the ultra-romantic and passionate
Throne of Judar miniseries,
available in July 2008.
Only from Silhouette Desire!

THOROUGHBRED LEGACY
*The stakes are high when it comes to love,
horse racing, family secrets
and broken promises.*

*A new exciting Harlequin continuity series
coming soon!*
Led by New York Times *bestselling author
Elizabeth Bevarly*
FLIRTING WITH TROUBLE

Here's a preview!

THE DOOR CLOSED behind them, throwing them into darkness and leaving them utterly alone. And the next thing Daniel knew, he heard himself saying, "Marnie, I'm sorry about the way things turned out in Del Mar."

She said nothing at first, only strode across the room and stared out the window beside him. Although he couldn't see her well in the darkness—he still hadn't switched on a light... but then, neither had she—he imagined her expression was a little preoccupied, a little anxious, a little confused.

Finally, very softly, she said, "Are you?"

He nodded, then, worried she wouldn't be able to see the gesture, added, "Yeah. I am. I should have said goodbye to you."

"Yes, you should have."

Actually, he thought, there were a lot of things he should have done in Del Mar. He'd had *a lot* riding on the Pacific Classic, and even more on his entry, Little Joe, but after meeting Marnie, the Pacific Classic had been the last thing on Daniel's mind. His loss at Del Mar had pretty much ended his career before it had even begun, and he'd had to start all over again, rebuilding from nothing.

He simply had not then and did not now have room in his life for a woman as potent as Marnie Roberts. He was a horseman first and foremost. From the time he was a school boy, he'd known what he wanted to do with his life—be the best possible trainer he could be.

He had to make sure Marnie understood—and he understood, too—why things had ended the way they had eight years ago. He just wished he could find the words to do that. Hell, he wished he could find the *thoughts* to do that.

"You made me forget things, Marnie, things that I really needed to remember. And that scared the hell out of me. Little Joe should have won the Classic. He was by far the best horse entered in that race. But I didn't give him the attention he needed and deserved that week, because all I could think about was you. Hell, when I woke up that morning all I wanted to do was lie there and look at you, and then wake you up and make love to you again. If I hadn't left when I did—the way I did—I might still be lying there in that bed with you thinking about nothing else."

"And would that be so terrible?" she asked.

"Of course not," he told her. "But that wasn't why I was in Del Mar," he repeated. "I was in Del Mar to win a race. That was my job. And my work was the most important thing to me."

She said nothing for a moment, only studied his face in the darkness as if looking for the answer to a very important question. Finally she asked, "And what's the most important thing to you now, Daniel?"

Wasn't the answer to that obvious? "My work," he answered automatically.

She nodded slowly. "Of course," she said softly. "That is after all, what you do best."

Her comment, too, puzzled him. She made it sound as if being good at what he did was a bad thing.

She bit her lip thoughtfully, her eyes fixed on his, glimmering in the scant moonlight that was filtering through the window. And damned if Daniel didn't find himself wanting to pull her into his arms and kiss her. But as much as it might have felt as if no time had passed since Del Mar, there were eight years between now and then. And eight years was a long time in the best of circumstances. For Daniel and Marnie, it was virtually a lifetime.

So Daniel turned and started for the door, then halted. He couldn't just walk away and leave things as they were, unsettled. He'd done that eight years ago and regretted it.

"It *was* good to see you again, Marnie," he said softly. And since he was being honest, he added, "I hope we see each other again."

She didn't say anything in response, only stood silhouetted against the window with her arms wrapped around her in a way that made him wonder whether she was doing it because she was cold, or if she just needed something—someone— to hold on to. In either case, Daniel understood. There was an emptiness clinging to him that he suspected would be there for a long time.

* * * * *

THOROUGHBRED LEGACY
coming soon wherever books are sold!

Thoroughbred Legacy

Launching in June 2008

A dramatic new 12-book continuity that embodies the American Dream.

Meet the Prestons, owners of Quest Stables, a successful horse-racing and breeding empire. But the lives, loves and reputations of this hardworking family are put at risk when a breeding scandal unfolds.

Flirting with Trouble

by *New York Times* bestselling author

ELIZABETH BEVARLY

Eight years ago, publicist Marnie Roberts spent seven days of bliss with Australian horse trainer Daniel Whittleson. But just as quickly, he disappeared. Now Marnie is heading to Australia to finally confront the man she's never been able to forget.

The stakes are high when it comes to love, horse racing, family secrets and broken promises.

A new exciting Harlequin continuity series coming soon!

HT38984R

Cole's Red-Hot Pursuit

Cole Westmoreland is a man who gets what he
wants. And he wants independent and sultry
Patrina Forman! She resists him—until a Montana
blizzard traps them together. For three delicious
nights, Cole indulges Patrina with his brand of
seduction. When the sun comes out, Cole and
Patrina are left to wonder—will this be the end of
the passion that storms between them?

Look for

COLE'S RED-HOT
PURSUIT

by USA TODAY bestselling author

BRENDA
JACKSON

Available in June 2008 wherever you buy books.

Always Powerful, Passionate and Provocative.

REQUEST YOUR FREE BOOKS!

2 FREE NOVELS PLUS 2 FREE GIFTS!

Silhouette® Desire®

Passionate, Powerful, Provocative!

YES! Please send me 2 FREE Silhouette Desire® novels and my 2 FREE gifts (gifts are worth about $10). After receiving them, if I don't wish to receive any more books, I can return the shipping statement marked "cancel". If I don't cancel, I will receive 6 brand-new novels every month and be billed just $4.05 per book in the U.S. or $4.74 per book in Canada, plus 25¢ shipping and handling per book and applicable taxes, if any*. That's a savings of almost 15% off the cover price! I understand that accepting the 2 free books and gifts places me under no obligation to buy anything. I can always return a shipment and cancel at any time. Even if I never buy another book, the two free books and gifts are mine to keep forever.

225 SDN ERVX 326 SDN ERVM

Name	(PLEASE PRINT)	
Address		Apt. #
City	State/Prov.	Zip/Postal Code

Signature (if under 18, a parent or guardian must sign)

Mail to the **Silhouette Reader Service:**
IN U.S.A.: P.O. Box 1867, Buffalo, NY 14240-1867
IN CANADA: P.O. Box 609, Fort Erie, Ontario L2A 5X3

Not valid to current subscribers of Silhouette Desire books.

Want to try two free books from another line?
Call 1-800-873-8635 or visit www.morefreebooks.com.

* Terms and prices subject to change without notice. N.Y. residents add applicable sales tax. Canadian residents will be charged applicable provincial taxes and GST. Offer not valid in Quebec. This offer is limited to one order per household. All orders subject to approval. Credit or debit balances in a customer's account(s) may be offset by any other outstanding balance owed by or to the customer. Please allow 4 to 6 weeks for delivery. Offer available while quantities last.

Your Privacy: Silhouette Books is committed to protecting your privacy. Our Privacy Policy is available online at www.eHarlequin.com or upon request from the Reader Service. From time to time we make our lists of customers available to reputable third parties who may have a product or service of interest to you. If you would prefer we not share your name and address, please check here. ☐

SDES08R

Royal Seductions

Michelle Celmer delivers a powerful miniseries in
Royal Seductions; where two brothers fight for the
crown and discover love. In *The King's Convenient Bride*,
the king discovers his marriage of convenience to the
woman he's been promised to wed is turning all too
real. The playboy prince proposes a mock engagement
to defuse rumors circulating about him and restore
order to the kingdom...until his pretend fiancée
becomes pregnant in *The Illegitimate Prince's Baby*.

Look for

THE KING'S CONVENIENT BRIDE

&

THE ILLEGITIMATE PRINCE'S BABY

BY MICHELLE CELMER

Available in June 2008 wherever you buy books.

Always Powerful, Passionate and Provocative.

COMING NEXT MONTH

#1873 JEALOUSY & A JEWELLED PROPOSITION—
Yvonne Lindsay
Diamonds Down Under
Determined to avenge his family's name, this billionaire sets out
to take over his biggest competition...and realizes his ex may be
the perfect weapon for revenge.

#1874 COLE'S RED-HOT PURSUIT—Brenda Jackson
After a night of passion, a wealthy sheriff will stop at nothing to
get the woman back into his bed. And he always gets what he wants.

#1875 SEDUCED BY THE ENEMY—Sara Orwig
Platinum Grooms
He has a score to settle with his biggest business rival. Seducing
his enemy's daughter proves to be the perfect way to have his
revenge.

#1876 THE KING'S CONVENIENT BRIDE—
Michelle Celmer
Royal Seductions
An arranged marriage turns all too real when the king falls for his
convenient wife. Don't miss the second book in the series, also
available this June!

#1877 THE ILLEGITIMATE PRINCE'S BABY—
Michelle Celmer
Royal Seductions
The playboy prince proposes a mock engagement...until his
pretend fiancée becomes pregnant! Don't miss the first book in
this series, also on sale this June!

#1878 RICH MAN'S FAKE FIANCÉE—Catherine Mann
The Landis Brothers
Caught in a web of tabloid lies, their only recourse is a fake
engagement. But the passion they feel for one another is all
too real.

SDCNM0508